LOOK OUT FOR THE
LITTLE GUY

LOOK OUT FOR THE
LITTLE GUY

SCOTT LANG

WITH ROB KUTNER

HYPERION
AVENUE

LOS ANGELES   NEW YORK

First Edition, September 2023
10 9 8 7 6 5 4 3 2 1
FAC-004510-23194
Printed in the United States of America

Designed by Stephanie Sumulong

Library of Congress Control Number: 2023932750
ISBN: 978-1-368-09013-1
Reinforced binding

www.HyperionAvenueBooks.com

Logo Applies to Text Stock Only

TO MY TWO FAVORITE PARTNERS:
HOPE AND CASSIE, THIS ONE'S FOR YOU!

INTRODUCTION

HI THERE. HOWDY. HEYA! Man, I hate introductions.

If you're reading this book, first of all, thank you! Even though I can make my body as large as the Empire State Building, some days my self-esteem gets, well, ant-sized. Maybe that's an occupational hazard of being an Avenger and working alongside the mightiest and smartest people on Earth, but the feeling is still there. Even when I remember that I did help save half the world.

Anyway, my name is Scott Lang. You may now or at one time have known me as "Ant-Man." I've been involved in some Super Hero stuff you might have heard about, some Super Hero stuff you probably haven't heard about, and some Super Hero stuff you might be tired of hearing about—at least if you're anything like my immediate family.

But who *is* Scott Lang? Well, I'm just an average, middle-aged white guy who went to a fancy nerd college, got married, and landed a solid white-collar desk job. I used to work as a computer guy at VistaCorp, a huge tech firm that deals with security. (Oh, the irony of that, but just wait for it!) My wife Maggie and I had a baby girl named Cassie, and we were heading into an uncomplicated, peaceful suburban life outside of San Francisco.

I mean, sure, on our TVs we were watching the world occasionally coming under attack by strange beings. But we also saw this amazing group of Super Heroes called the Avengers, who always managed to show up exactly when they were needed and send those baddies back . . . away. From our planet. And my life.

However, there were still some baddies right here on Earth. Specifically, in my workplace.

As I began to discover over time, my company was not completely on the up-and-up. Under the (mis)guidance of my boss, the company I was working at, VistaCorp, started using its prowess with security to take advantage of customers. Specifically, someone either overlooked or deliberately created a glitch in the payment-processing software, skimming millions of dollars from customer accounts.

I decided I was not okay with that.

After multiple attempts to push back against the company, attempts that one might describe as "legal" or "reasonable" or "advisable," I decided to go in a different direction.

I'd like to start with the positives: I returned five million dollars to our customers and exposed VistaCorp's nefarious dealings to the public.

And, on the other side, I also drove an extremely expensive sports car into an extremely expensive pool, and myself into San Quentin Federal Penitentiary for three years.

Even worse, this was also around the time that my marriage to Maggie broke up. I don't want to get into the specifics of why—that's strictly Scott-Maggie stuff—but let's just say "Husband suddenly going to the pen for three years" wasn't exactly a marriage-saver.

More critically, though, that divorce, plus imprisonment, effectively separated me from my dear, sweet daughter, Cassie. For way too many of her precious first few years. I wondered if she and I would ever even have the chance to make a connection.

Eventually, I finished my sentence, left San Q, and attempted to rejoin the world. Even if the world didn't quite seem to know what to do with me yet. I couldn't get a job with a conviction on my record. I had no funds or place to stay. Even my one joyful attempt to reunite with Cassie was cut short by Maggie and her fiancé, telling me I had to get my life together before we could talk visitation or shared custody.

Fortunately, though, there was one guy who did have a use for me.

Unless you've spent the past few years in a cave (or, say, a subatomic realm), you've probably at least heard of Pym Technologies. Or at least, Hank Pym.

If you haven't, Hank Pym was the inventor of the Pym Particle, an incredible scientific breakthrough. Pym Particles have the power to cause molecular reduction or expansion at great scales in either direction. In other words, they can make anything super-small or super-big. Hank and his wife, Janet Van Dyne, put this to direct use on themselves, performing countless heroic deeds as the original Ant-Man and The Wasp.

And outside of the Super Hero game, Hank started a serious R&D operation known as Pym Technologies.

But a few years ago, Pym Tech fell into the unscrupulous hands of people who wanted to exploit his discoveries for use on the battlefield—and to sell the resulting technology to folks we really do *not* want to be in battle with! By then, Hank had been pushed out of the company that literally had his last name on the door. But he knew what was being planned with his invention, and that it had to be stopped. So he . . . let's say "hired" me to recover his creations from Pym Tech.

Whoa, whoa, whoa, Scott! is probably what you're saying right now. *How did we jump from custody disputes to biotech espionage?*

Well, right about the time I was stumbling out of prison, trying to find myself, Hank Pym—whom I didn't know at the time—found me. Hank had done his research on me and knew I was skilled at both electronics and thievery. And most importantly, he knew that I had nothing left to lose.

Unbeknownst to me, he "tested" me by enticing me to steal the Ant-Man suit from his highly formidable safe. Once I succeeded at that, Hank and his daughter, Hope Van Dyne, kinda "stole" me from police custody, offered me the gig (as if I had a choice!), and then trained me to pull off one of the craziest high-tech heists ever.

So, return the potentially world-threatening military

technology to its rightful creator, and it's back to peace again, right?

Wrong.

Literally no sooner had I pulled off the Pym Tech operation (with an assist from some old prison pals and some extremely skilled ants) than I found myself face-to-face with the Avengers.

Well, two of them, anyway. Captain America and the Falcon. Believe me, two's more than enough!

I'd already had a tussle with the Falcon, but now he and Cap (as I would soon be calling him, no big deal) actually wanted *my help*.

Wow. I mean, wow! It wasn't just cranky old semi-retired scientists tracking me down anymore—now I'd caught the attention of Earth's Mightiest.

So what they wanted me for was . . . a bit messy. Basically, the Avengers had a huge internal divide over something too complicated to get into here, and Cap and Falcon wanted some fresh (and highly size-adaptable) muscle on their side. Especially when all of this culminated in a huge Avengers-vs.-Avengers fracas at an airport in Germany. Germany! I'd just spent three years in a tiny cell. Now I was suddenly "doing Europe"?

I don't want to get into the details of the conflict (and in fact I am under legal obligation not to), but let's just say I might have been on the more "badass" side of it.

In the end, that whole fight got resolved, as I think you know. Otherwise our planet would be a scorched battlefield of never-ending intra-Avengers smackdowns.

So . . . peace on Earth *now*?

Nope. That's when—thanks to Thanos—half of all life in the universe disappeared. So no, no peace on Earth or anywhere else.

I wasn't around for those five years of missing people (you'll find out why soon), but I came back just in time, jumped to a different timeline, fought, like, every bad guy in the universe on a field in upstate New York, helped the Avengers stop Thanos, and put all the people back where they belonged. Including, last but not least, putting my precious Hope back together with me!

As you might imagine, that was . . . *a lot.*

So in the time since, I've been trying to take things a bit easier. Nursing wounds. Reconnecting with those I've missed. Reflecting on what it all means.

Oh yes, and of course, writing this book!

And if you want to *really* get to know who Scott Lang is, reading this book is where I'd recommend you start.

So at this point, I bet you also have a very serious question—one which I've asked myself over a thousand times a day while writing this:

Why on Earth is Scott Lang *the first Super Hero writing a book?*

I mean, just between us, I'm proud to be an Avenger, but sometimes I also feel like a "latecomer." Sure, I came through in the ultimate clutch, but in baseball terms, I'm not a starter—I'm a DH (designated hero).

Here's how I see it: I'm the "everyman Avenger." I'm the one you could grab a beer with, the one you'd feel okay asking to look after your dog when you're away or for a drive to the airport. I'm not a Super Soldier or a billionaire (unless this book is super-successful), just a regular dad, a San Francisco Giants fan, and a guy who's made mistakes I'm still trying to rectify.

In a word, I'm an ordinary guy who's been thrust—more than once—into extraordinary circumstances.

And I know that still doesn't completely answer the question of why I wrote this book.

The simple answer is, "The Avengers asked me to."

One day, Bruce "the Hulk" Banner and Clint "Hawkeye" Barton took me out for lunch. They said they were concerned that the world didn't really *know* what had happened with Thanos and the Blip and our long struggle to finally put things right again.

At first, as I usually do when confronted with heavy

topics, I made a joke: "I'm pretty sure at least half the world knows what happened."

Bruce responded that yes, of course, billions had *experienced* these jarring and mind-bending events, but they didn't know the full story behind them. And ultimately, that's what people need the most to get through and get past traumatic events: a narrative that helps it all make sense.

"Okay," I agreed. "Solid plan. So who are you going to get to tell that story?"

Clint answered, "You, Scott. You're the guy who got scooped up in all this pretty recently. You've still got one foot in their world. And you're a guy everyone likes . . . and trusts."

And Bruce sealed the deal: "It's tough stuff, and no one knows how to keep it light like you."

Well. I still had tons of doubts. I was hardly an eyewitness to almost all that history. I hadn't been around for the Battle of Wakanda, or any of the events that led to Thanos gathering the various Infinity Stones.

But pretty much immediately, I knew what my answer would be. As far as I'm concerned, when the Avengers ask you do to a job—any job—you say yes. So I did. Two quick handshakes (Bruce—now permanently in his Hulk body—made sure to keep his "not *too* firm"), and it was settled. They'd supply me all the archival footage and documentation, take me anywhere I needed to go, and let me ask as many questions as I needed.

The only thing is, it wasn't actually 100 percent settled for me—on the inside. From the confidence peak of having two amazing Super Heroes place their trust in you, there was a frighteningly steep plummet into self-doubt. Even with their sensible reasons, the whole affair just stirred up a question that's been burning inside me most of my adult life:

Why me?

I've been asking myself that since before I even met the Avengers. Back when I was working at VistaCorp, why was I the only one who couldn't sleep at night after learning of all the money they were stealing from customers? Why did I basically give up my job, give up my marriage, and spend three years in San Quentin, just so I could play Robin Hood?

And finally—and this one still smarts—when VistaCorp's nasty business became public to the world, why was I the one who ended up going down for it?

I don't know the answers to these questions. And perhaps I never will.

Not even Doctor Strange can tell me, and believe me, it's not for my lack of asking. Once the purple dust had settled from the Battle of Earth, I tried bonding with the guy. Let's just say, he was either unwilling or uninterested in filling me in about any of my 14,000,605 possible pasts.

But here's what I do know. That VistaCorp/prison experience taught me that our world is broken. And that it's never going to get fixed unless folks like me—the *unlikely ones*—step up to the job.

And when Hank Pym plucked me out of the ex-con pool and put me to work as Ant-Man 2.0, I started to see the haziest outlines of a "why" for me. Maybe all those hard years I had just endured were actually preparation for a higher purpose.

Which is a good thing, because right after my first outing as a hero, I was drafted into that aforementioned very scary and sort of confusing business with Avengers fighting other Avengers in Germany, I was sent to an underwater super-SUPER-max prison, and once again, I had to take the fall and spend two more years in detention under house arrest.

Why me again?

Still no perfect lock on the answer, but I was beginning

to glimpse one. This is going to sound beyond weird for a guy whose success—and often life—depends on quantum mechanics, but basically, I had a *feeling*.

Even as I was yanked from one seemingly unthinkable scenario to another, asked to do things I would have never dreamed possible, I began to see that many incredible things *were*, in fact, possible—and I was doing them. And they started to feel more and more, for lack of a better word, *right*.

I know this is the kind of feeling my Avengers pals feel mid-mission or mid-battle, and maybe they've gotten used to it, but I'm just finally getting there. To the feeling that, even when faced with the most terrifying foes imaginable, even with the odds exponentially stacked against you, if you are working side by side with others to serve a greater good, you are in the right place, doing the right thing. For *you*.

And honestly, that's the real story behind the entire Avengers saga. It's the one I thought was most essential to share with all of you. That was the deeper reason I said yes to those two Avengers at the lunch counter. Because I knew that, once again, I was being called to do what seemed impossible (or at least, highly inadvisable)—but instead, I let the feeling take hold, and guide me.

And I realized that I needed to share that feeling with you.

Because at the end of the day, *nobody* can tell where life is going to yank them, unexpectedly and seemingly beyond their reach. Steve Rogers signed up to fight, imagining he'd only go as far as a scrawny guy can get in wartime. Tony Stark was brilliant and successful, but I know a part of him wondered if he'd ever get out from under his dad's shadow. Even Doctor Strange in all his professional success could never have imagined becoming a Master of the Mystic Arts—or even that such a thing existed!

And that same unpredictability is just as true for you as it is for me. What would you do if life shrunk you down and tossed you into a bathtub being filled by your former prison buddy? Okay, that one might just be me. But how about when life sends you unexpectedly packing from your gig of three years and straight into a jail cell—because you dared to blow the whistle on your company's greed?

You don't ask why. You ask, "Where do I go from here?"

Because *that's the job life has for you*, at least right at this moment, and it's the kind of job you don't get to quit.

You can run, but you can't hide—not even if you *can* shrink yourself down and leap into a bathtub.

Now I know I said before that I don't, technically, have a super-power. But looked at another way, I actually do. And the even cooler part is, so do all of you.

Having the ability to change my size at will, I've seen that the world is full of "big guys" and "little guys." And unsurprisingly, the former is always stepping on the latter. Sometimes this is by design, but sometimes, just because of their status and drive, the big folks don't even see the everyday, hard-working folks just trying to get by.

That's why it's always the job of people like me—and, as I'm going to show you throughout this book, *you*—to look out for the little guy. That's something we all have a super-powered ability to do, if we simply choose to accept the job.

You are in this place and time for a reason, and no one else is. And so—when that next uncertain, unlikely, "impossible" step is revealed to you—I urge you with every particle in my body, Pym or otherwise, to turn that "Why me?" into a "Why *not* me?"

At least that's what I tried to do when I promised the Avengers I would tell their story. And the best way I know how to do that is by telling mine at the same time. Because as I've learned, whenever I start to talk about something big that happened, I also see the little lessons that can be learned from it, and I want to share that, to help myself and others.

Maybe it's because I didn't get the chance to be around my daughter Cassie for so many chunks of her life, to share what I'd learned with her. I'm still working on that, but it's hard now that she's a grown-up herself who's

All right, you handsome devil, let's read this book you've written.

already seen and experienced so much without me to guide her. I missed the boat on that one, but believe me, you are in for an entire book of "Dad wisdom" just burning for a home.

So that's what I plan to do in this book. I'm going to tell it all, from how I saw it, experienced it, and heard it firsthand from my hero buddies. I'm going to bring you into the hero world.

Along the way, you'll hear about *my* story—Scott Lang's story—from where I started to the (ant-) man I've become, and am still becoming. Because I'm so incredibly fascinating? No. Because my life—just like yours—loses half its value if we don't find a way to share its lessons with others.

And finally, because—if you take nothing else away from my words—what I want to share is that what makes *all* of us giants is how much we look out for the little guy. How we help out our fellow humans when they need it most. How our greatest super-power can simply be a listening ear, a concerned eye, or an outstretched hand. How we don the "hero's uniform" by simply showing up and doing the unbelievably unlikely job that life has just handed us.

And speaking of jobs, I've got an entire rest of a book to write. Oh, why did I agree to this? *WHY ME?*

REDOS & REDON'TS

SOME PEOPLE SAY THE hardest thing in life is starting something.

But I say, it's starting all over again.

There's a famous Chinese proverb, usually attributed to Lao-Tzu, that goes, "The journey of a thousand miles begins with a single step." But in my relatively short lifetime, I've had my share of wipe-the-slate-clean-I-got-nothin' "restarts."

For instance, have you ever been released from prison? One day you're on a schedule of people telling you what to do 24/7, the next, you're so helpless, it's like a second infancy: Don't know where to go, where to live, and no one will hire you for work. And in my case, there wasn't even family to return to. My ex was remarrying, and to my young daughter I was more like a rumor than an actual person.

And then, of course, there was trying to get my bearings after returning from the Quantum Realm. That was already strange enough, just being back in a place where things like "time" and "matter" and "Scott's brain" work in a way I am used to.

Now add in the fact that, in what seemed like just a few hours to me, *years* had apparently passed for the rest of the world! I know, I know, this doesn't even compare to the experience all of you had going through it, in real time. I can't even imagine what that was like, having half the world—and probably half the people you care about—just disappear! It's a lot for anyone to wrap their heads around, but I'm going to try a little later in the book.

At that moment, though, this indescribable wave of human loss was only starting to hit me with full force. I was five years behind the rest of the world just trying to process it.

Then it suddenly got super-personal. As I soon came to learn, my newly adopted family—Hank, Hope, and Janet—were also no more.

The one saving grace was that I got my daughter Cassie back. But once again, I'd lost yet another few years of her already-growing-up-too-fast life!

And finally, there was of course my new "work family"—the Avengers. Awesome role models and, I'd like to think, friends.

But what made things extra disorienting for me at this moment was just a supreme confusion over who I was and what I was supposed to be. I was someone who'd *just* reinvented himself from "ex-con" to "hero guy." And now I walked into a world where I'd completely missed out on the chance to be a hero and stop literally the biggest threat to humankind of all time.

My point is, in multiple situations, I've had to hit the reset button on my own life. And every single time, no matter how many times you do it, it's hard. And it's scary. We humans tend to get addicted to the familiar, even in nearly intolerable situations. We cling like hell to what we know. So what happens when those things disappear and we're left flailing in midair with nothing to cling to?

I'll get into this in more detail in a second, but basically, we have to find a new, unexplored part of ourselves to latch on to. That's how we climb back up into being a new us in a new world.

I'm seeing a lot of this fear and confusion right now among my friends. With the existential threat of Thanos behind us, a bunch of my hero peers are just learning, for the first time, how to move on. Whether it's passing the torch (or hammer, or shield, or bow and arrow) to someone new—or, like Hope, trading in the Wasp suit for a corporate pantsuit. For me, all I'm trying to focus on right now is finishing this book. And when I'm done, I'll certainly be trying to figure out my own next chapter.

But here's the surprising part: Having been around this existential merry-go-round a few times now, *this* time I'm actually kind of psyched for the wild and unpredictable ride awaiting me next.

What's my secret? Well, you know the old cliché "When life gives you lemons, make lemonade"?

That cliché wants to force you to create your next move out of what you've been given. But there's one very important word in there that's often ignored: *YOU*.

In other words, forget the lemons. Life has already given you a *you* that's like no other. And that's what you're better off making stuff out of.

But how do you find that "you" to build on? Based on my experiences, I've broken it into two steps:

1. ALLOW YOURSELF TO MOURN WHAT'S GONE.

Bawl your eyes out! This is really key to the whole "you-finding" process, because it helps clarify what part of you was tied up in other people and things, and what lives on. And it needs to be said out loud, because a lot of people think that shedding a single tear will dissolve their defenses.

I can't tell you, after I emerged from the Quantum Realm into a post-Blip world, how many nights I soaked my pillow with tears.

And all of that, of course, reminds me of what I missed coming out of prison: too much of my little girl's childhood. Don't get me wrong, we had a lot of good times later on, but I can never, ever get those years back.

How sad can you be about losing something you never had? Turns out, very.

Just remember one thing, though: Tears are acidic, which means they dissolve stuff. But not just chemically—spiritually. They don't dissolve your strength. *They dissolve the glue that keeps you sealed into an earlier version of yourself.* The idea that "I can only be me with one specific group of people, in one specific context."

But if you think about it, your whole life—indeed, everyone's—moves through a mind-boggling variety of situations and people. Nothing stays the same. Nobody sticks around forever. So we have a choice: We can spend our lives clinging to what we know, or we can grab as many memories as possible and move on to what's new and maybe even better ahead of us. And sometimes the noise of that decision to move ahead can be quite loud and painful.

So I say embrace the tears. Be loud, be proud, be soggy, and let it all out. Because yes, loss hurts. But so do most things that make you better. Don't dam up that flood, let it roll over you, because in the end it will wash you clean. Not of the past—just the voice telling you to stay there.

2. FIGURE OUT HOW TO REBUILD.

I know what you're thinking: *Easy for you to say, Scott. You're an Avenger. You probably have tons of resources at your disposal. You could pull off a "full redo" after every major event in your life.* But what I'm talking about is not changing your physical circumstances. I mean rebuilding *the idea of what you're capable of*—You 2.0. Or 3.0 or 4.0—wherever you are on your journey.

So how do you do that? The first, and probably most crucial, step is: Separate out what you and others say you

Yes, Hank really did me a solid with this whole Ant-Man gig.
But did he have to make the suit so *heavy*?

are from what you can do. Shift your focus from adjectives to verbs. When I first came out of the slammer, recruiters called me "unemployable," and my ex-wife Maggie called me "unreliable." Ouch. But ultimately, those are just descriptors, and descriptors can change.

By contrast, through his actions, Hank Pym told me that I was *really good* at sneaking in and stealing things.

Not the world's best compliment, I admit. Even if that's about the highest praise anyone ever gets from Hank Pym. But Hank had a clear purpose behind that clear-eyed assessment of me. He wanted me to steal for a *good* reason, and he wanted the guy who's best at it. Over time, Hank showed me how to find that "best guy" within me. By redirecting who I already was into a guy who still snuck in and stole things, but in a different way and for a nobler cause.

And you know what? Hank was right. I *was* good at "stealing for good"! Even when I fumbled at recovering the Space Stone during the Time Heist (don't worry, all those words will make sense soon), it's only because Loki was *better* at stealing. Not that I'm bad at it. But we're talking *Loki*—not a fair comparison.

In brief, I took the worst thing about me and found a way to do that thing for a better cause.

Likewise, when I came out of the Quantum Realm and found half the planet gone, at first I was consumed with one unanswerable question. Why was *I* spared, when so many weren't? I quickly got locked into describing myself as "unworthy." You see? More of those unhelpful—and paralyzing—"descriptors."

Fortunately, I didn't have the luxury of wallowing in those feelings. And frankly, no one even wanted to hear it. I was five years behind everyone else who had already endured enough pain going through this.

I was experiencing a common psychological feeling: survivor's guilt.

But eventually, I started to shift my perspective and rethink that term—starting with the descriptor. I mean, "guilt"? The only person even calling me guilty for surviving Thanos was me.

So I redirected my focus onto the "survivor" part. That transformed my thinking. Now I began to tell myself, "I'm good at surviving. How can I bring more of *that* into the world?" That's what drove my mind back to the time shenanigans I'd observed in the Quantum Realm, and that's what made me crash Avengers Compound.

So, to take a step back, how does someone who has lost everything achieve a "redo"? The key to a "redo" is the "do." You rebuild your life—and sometimes re-rebuild it, and sometimes even re-re-rebuild it—by embracing these three facts:

You are so much more than who you "were." Especially as you get further away from what shaped you in the past.

You aren't limited by who you are. Or at least the way others describe you.

You are what you can do. To rebuild is to take what you know how to do—no matter how unconventional or questionable that skill might seem to you now—and figure out how to do it differently. How to use it to take your life in a new direction. A better one.

FAAMQ

(Frequently Asked Ant-Man Questions)

AS A SUPER HERO, I meet a lot of people. People with a lot of questions. And here's the funny (but sometimes annoying) thing: They're very often *the exact same handful of questions*. And it's never the one I really want to hear: "Will you take a picture with my dog?"

Even though an ant's jaw is famously strong, my human jaw sometimes gets tired of answering the same things over and over. So to help all my fans (and my poor mandible), I thought I'd include my most frequently asked questions and answers throughout this book. Aren't I thoughtful that way?

Q: *I know you can shrink down to quantum size, but is there a limit to how big you can get?*

A: To be perfectly honest, that's one of those Hank Pym questions that I hate to ask him, because he takes everything as a critique: "Oh, so it doesn't get big enough for you now? Why do you need to be bigger?"

But seriously, from what I've experienced, self-enlargement is something any user of the Ant-Man or the Wasp suit needs to be *really* careful with. For a variety of reasons, it takes a big toll on the human body. Or at least mine. For one thing, going big puts a strain on my nervous system. So if my size hits a certain threshold, I start to see things. Like, specifically, the ground coming toward me. Fast!

MAKING YOUR
HOUSE ARREST . . .
A *HOME* ARREST

ANOTHER QUESTION I GET asked a lot—one that takes a bit longer to answer—is "Scott, what did you *do* while trapped in your house for two years?"

This is going to sound beyond ironic, but those two years sequestered under house arrest (my sentence for joining some Avengers who were on the wrong side of the law) were some of the freest of my life.

Here's a few ways I found that freedom.

JAILHOUSE ROCKING

I wasn't expecting to get any life lessons from prison, other than "how to survive." But looking back, I can tell you one thing I learned: how to free up my mind and create a whole life out of limited space and mobility. And I brought that freedom to my new digs.

For example, the freedom to completely *mix up your routine.* Go to sleep standing up! Brush your teeth *before* you eat! For no good reason at all, set your watch to Tokyo time. Have breakfast for dinner, or—even more shockingly—dinner for breakfast!

These may sound like nothing more than quirky "lifestyle tweaks," but what I now realize I was doing was breaking out of a different kind of prison. I had come to let not only jail, but indeed the whole notion of being an "ex-con," define me. Restrict me from becoming more. And I was hungering to free myself up to become that something more. But with any big change it's always wisest to start with the small stuff.

And finally, those three years behind bars made me appreciate getting outside every chance I could. In the slammer, if I was lucky I'd get thirty minutes "on the yard" every day, which meant thirty minutes living in fear of getting my butt kicked every day. So after that experience, I spent every minute I could outside trying to keep my tiny pathetic garden from becoming a delphinium graveyard.

Wow, Scott, gardening—mind blown! I know, I know, but my point is, I'd lived in Northern California, surrounded by places of epic natural beauty, and ignored them. But now, in a little three-foot-by-six-foot patch of dirt, I finally found my connection to the planet I was so often fighting to save.

MAN CAVING

Did you know you can order literally *anything* delivered to your home? (Except, it turns out, a key to an ankle monitor?) Of course you did, and our world is adorned with massive piles of cardboard boxes as tall as Stark Tower to prove it. That is why I tried to limit my purchases, and was extremely selective with what I ordered. I guided my decisions by one thoughtful, ironclad purchasing principle: *What will eat up the most time?*

Naturally, that meant starting with a gaming console. But to really get the most out of the experience—one of the new habits I was trying to pick up while confined—no matter how frustrated I got, I would never ever use a cheat code. Another good life lesson right there.

I also expanded my interests: learning close-up magic online, reading books I'd always meant to, singing karaoke—something that pre-house-arrest Scott was "too cool" for. But now, though penned in by walls, I was determined to no longer stay penned in by old ways of seeing myself.

Another consideration was: *What will best keep my sanity intact?* Now that I was barred by an international body from fighting bad guys, I needed *something* to pound on. So I decided to learn the drums.

This was not only cathartic, it had an added sanity-preserving bonus: When I really cranked it up, my noises were disturbing enough to get neighbors yelling into my windows, "Keep it down!" or "I'm trying to sleep!" or "Learn a second song!"

Yes! Human connection!

And attempting to entertain guests in my man cave was always . . . interesting. I'm not a total slob, but also not a fan of cleaning. Let's just say when people ask how I decorated my place, my answer is "Not."

Also, since being kicked out by Maggie and living as a tenant of the state, I didn't really have any cookware of my own. Other than a lot of items I ordered to make food "for one." Is there any phrase in the English language sadder than "Single-Serving Cake-Maker"?

Long story short, I started getting lonely. And I'm the type of guy who needs other people around or I start talking to myself. And that gets even sadder, real quick. So another way I began to reorient my life was toward that important need. Really, the most important one of all.

KEEPING UP WHILE KEEPING IN

I've already mentioned the lack of a "normal" social life when an ankle-bracelet has turned you into a permanent homebody. But here again, I found that confinement freed me up in an unexpected way.

In the past, I somehow never found the time or energy to build and nurture deeper connections with friends. Admittedly, I had never had the most bandwidth for staying on top of my friends' lives. And that only got worse as I got wrapped up in marriage and having a kid.

But now, freed of any demands on my time or energy, life had thrown me the keys to go "outside my bubble" and make an extra effort to maintain contact with everyone.

Before long, I had turned friendship from a lazy hobby into a disciplined habit. By the end of my stay, I had schedules, calendars, speed-dial settings. I kept in touch by every method available: calling, emailing, and even using some annoying videoconference platform, which I guess could catch on one day. For a guy who was always in one place, in my friends' lives I was everywhere.

And of course, the sweetest irony of all was that being stuck here meant I could get joyfully stuck with my favorite person of all. . . .

CASSIE-ING IT UP

House arrest literally gave me the opportunity of a lifetime: finally getting to hang with my precious Cassie! So much time to make up for! So many things I wanted to do with her!

But since we couldn't go out, I had to figure out how to replicate all those activities while still inside the house. Fortunately, even the minimal amount of deliveries I'd had still left with me a decent supply of delivery-box cardboard to work with. So that was the dawn of the Cardboard Roller Coaster, the Cardboard Robot War, the Cardboard Pony Ride, and in one ill-considered move, the Cardboard Waterpark.

One advantage of having a house decorated "bachelor-style" is that there's just about nothing for you to break or stain, and even if you do, no one will care. I didn't have Hope around to disapprove of my mess (which, I have to admit, gave me a slight twinge of sadness every time I made one). So instead, I leaned in to the other "special girl" in my life and gave her every inch of grubby floor I could.

Now despite what I said earlier about trying to kill time, with Cassie it was quite the opposite. Every second flew by faster than a magical hammer returning to Thor's hand. And I wanted so badly for it to slow down! Man, if only I had known about quantum tunneling then, I . . . still would have not wanted to open that can of wormholes.

Because as I was learning with Cassie, and all these other experiences, the worst way to live is to spend

If there's one thing that improves house arrest, it's a beloved family member—ideally of the under 10 variety, as shown here. (Also, note me styling that super-cool bathrobe!)

your life running away from your limitations. Instead, you have to learn how to embrace them, and transform them . . . and in the process, yourself.

It was part of a little something I call . . .

THE FREEDOM PARADOX

I know it sounds screwy. Under normal conditions, all day long I have nothing but options. I can basically *fly* (well, at least while riding an ant or catching a ride with Hope). I can also see anything macro or micro. And, not to put too fine a point on it, but right now I don't exactly have a day job.

But here's the thing: When you're pulled in all directions at all times, you can lose sight of what really matters in your life. Yes, your life is technically, physically free, but at the same time, you're not necessarily living *your life*. You're seeking comfort or avoiding pain, putting out fires, operating on muscle memory, and most of all, just plain getting distracted. You're a hamster on a wheel of your own making.

I know this because living in the same place, day in, day out, was the first thing in my decades of life that actually concentrated my mind on what I really wanted most, and how to get it. But it did even more than that. It focused my intentions on uncovering who I really was.

In my opinion, that's a critical quest all of us should go on—the one to find our truest self. The problem is, there are just too many other options pulling us away from it. But when I had most of those options removed, and had literally nowhere else to go, I was finally able to "go inside."

So you could say I spent those twenty-four months doing "nothing." Nothing *but* talking with friends (a lot!), learning to appreciate the simple blessings of my life, and trying new things—by which I really mean, trying out new versions of me. And of course, rollicking in pure joy with Cassie.

And you know what? That's not nothing.

That's *everything.*

FAAMQ

Q: *Besides having wings, is the Wasp suit the same as the Ant-Man one?*

A: First of all, I'm going to pause on that "besides," because I've still never gotten a good explanation from Hank about this obviously glaring injustice! He always mumbles some tech gibberish about "lift/drag issues," and then suddenly he "has a meeting."

But there are two main differences between the Wasp and Ant-Man suits that I'm aware of. One are these wrist-mounted gauntlets that can fire powerful blasters, which Hope has used in some key battles. The other difference, which I admittedly don't fully understand, is a more intuitive—as opposed to manual—control system. Basically, I have to use buttons to change size, whereas Hope can just control this feature with her mind.

This allows her to amplify her strength. And, considering how strong she is at normal size, let me just say: Do *not* mess with the tiny Wasp!

"MY DADDY, MY HERO"

BY CASSIE LANG
(PLUS A FEW NOTES FROM DADDY)

WHEN CASSIE WAS NINE years old, her third-grade teacher assigned the class to write an essay on "My Hero." Why am I including it in this book? Because I really wanted to include my little girl's perspective on some of the wild things happening to me that had a *huge* impact on her. Because I wanted her voice to be a part of all this, too. And finally . . . because it's actually a pretty riveting account of one of my first outings as Ant-Man! I mean, she does skip over a little backstory (like me stealing Hank Pym's Super

Hero suit and finding out Hank engineered all that to convince me to be Ant-Man and defeat Yellowjacket and his evil plans). But for a nine-year-old who wasn't there for all that other stuff, she does pretty great! Without further ado, here is my daughter's earliest magnum opus.

Mommy says Daddy is only supposed to visit me on certain days or weekends.[1] *But I want to tell you about the time that Daddy made a "surprise" visit and saved my life!*

It was a school night. I was in bed. Then there was a big CRASH, I heard Mommy scream, and suddenly there was a . . . giant bee guy in my bedroom! But not a cool-looking one like Ant-Man.[2] *He was an ugly-looking guy with extra legs and yellow stripes everywhere. He looked like if a giant robot-bee got splashed in mustard.*

I wanted to scream. But before I could even take a breath, Bee Guy (later Daddy told me his name was really "Yellowjacket") grabbed me! I was totally scared about being grabbed by a strange grown-up. Except then I stopped being scared when I saw how silly his costume was.[3]

---

1 Reminder to Daddy: Hire a better attorney!

2 My daughter is literally the only person on the planet who thinks this, but I'll take it! ☺

3 Let's just say the standards for Halloween in San Francisco are *high*.

I've seen good costumes in the comic books Daddy sent me. This was not a good costume. He said, "Don't be scared." I asked him, "Are you a monster?"[4]

He didn't really answer. All he said was, "Do I look like a monster?" Which is totally wrong, because Mommy always says, "Don't judge a book by its cover!" So I was about to say, "I only care if you're a monster on the inside," but all I said was "I want my daddy," and then Daddy showed up!

Well, Daddy and Bee Guy started fighting all around my bedroom. I wasn't even thinking about any of my toys getting broken, because I was more worried about Daddy getting broken.[5] *And then they got super-small, and suddenly the fight was happening on my toy train set! And then a whole army of ants showed up and started fighting alongside Daddy to stop Bee Guy.*

AND THEN, things went from small to big. And I mean my whole train set! Suddenly there was a giant train in the middle of my bedroom. And a giant ant!

That's when Mommy's boyfriend, Paxton, showed up with the police. I thought he was going to help, but Bee Guy's outfit was too powerful, and soon he had Paxton and me trapped!

---

4 One of the many things I love about this girl is how she *gets right to the point!*

5 Awwww. Also, she was not the only one with this fear!

The author of this essay, pictured at her most angelic.

And then the weirdest thing happened: Daddy just . . . disappeared![6]

Then Bee Guy started dancing around and yelling like something hurt, and he was hitting himself! And then he also disappeared! And then Daddy . . . reappeared.

---

6 Sadly, she probably has a lot of diary entries like this. . . .

I have no idea what happened at the end there. But Bee Guy was gone, regular-sized Daddy was back, and I was never going to stop hugging him ever again.

Hi! Daddy here again. I have to confess something. All those reasons I listed at the beginning about why I decided to include this essay in my book? None of those were the real one.

The truth is, I just love reading this little glimpse into my (formerly) little one's mind at this stage of her life. And not just because I missed out on so much of her childhood. Because, as she's gotten older, as often happens with dads and daughters (especially dads who've periodically gotten yanked out of those daughters' lives for long stretches and highly unpredictable reasons), things between us have gotten . . . complicated.

But it gives me life to remember a time that she did. And it also gives me hope that someday soon, she will again.

FAAMQ

Q: *You can talk to ants. But can they talk back to you?*

A: Well, I don't literally "speak" to them. My headset converts speech into electromagnetic waves that target the ants' olfactory centers, which is their main avenue of communication. A more accurate term would be that I can "electro-scent" messages to ants. And yes, I know, that does sound like something from a 1950s sci-fi movie.

So, to answer your question (kind of!), ants obviously don't have the same technology to "speak" back to me. At least not to my nose. But that doesn't mean they don't communicate. When I send my little buds a "smellogram," if they receive it and it works for them, they get right to it!

Ants actually get a ton of stuff done without saying a word. We could all learn a lesson from that.

ANT, INC.

FROM THE VERY FIRST moment I met Hank Pym, I could tell he was going to be an effective boss. Think about it: Without lifting a finger, the man got me released from jail, ensnared in his house, and dutifully carrying out probably the riskiest and most complicated heist ever (at least until the nabbing of the Infinity Stones).

What I didn't realize is that, along the way, he would teach me how to be a good leader, too.

It was, quite simply, a prerequisite for the mission

Hank had "recruited" me for. Some scary military folks had taken over Hank's former company, and they were threatening to use his designs to make even scarier military tech with it. We were going to stop that—by stealing it back.

There's no way we'd be able to break into such an uber-secure place without the help of Hank's elite ant squad. That meant that, first and foremost, I'd have to learn how to work effectively with them. And eventually, to lead them into battle.

So Hank started me on regular training sessions with my tiny future colleagues. (For the record, this was already on top of daily, physically exhausting combat training sessions with Hope. But that I didn't mind as much, because, you know, getting to be with Hope!)

Hank explained that even though his fancy, high-tech invention, the EMP Device, enabled humans to "speak" to ants (using electromagnetic waves to stimulate the olfactory centers in their brains that they use to communicate), it . . . wasn't that simple.

To truly take charge, he said, you have to prove to the ants that you can navigate the world as they do, alongside them at their scale, acting for all intents and purposes as if you *belonged* in the colony.

That was the final, somewhat abstract-sounding-to-me goal. And getting to that goal was a huge challenge.

Once I'd learned all about the bells and whistles of the Ant-Man suit, Hank instructed me to try joining the ants on their level. You know, "fitting in."

At first, I was a very, very bad fit.

I shrunk down to their size and dropped into an underground burrow in Hank's backyard, where I was to meet the so-called "Crazy Ant."

One of those apricot-colored fellows came right up to me like a friendly dog, jumping into my lap while I petted it. I thought, "Instant rapport! Scott, you're a natural ant-pal."

Then suddenly, its mates were all over me.

I don't know if they were defending their colleague or joining the cuddle party, but it freaked me out! I instantly jumped back to human size to escape.

Next up was an attempted meet-and-greet with a Bullet Ant, whose bite is exceptionally painful even to a full-sized human. Now I started imagining how that would feel on my head, which was currently slightly smaller than this guy's—and it was moving toward me, fast. Now it was almost on top of me. Now too "on top" for me to handle! I re-enlarged myself once again.

I wasn't exactly nailing the "show that you belong" side of things.

Finally, I started to make an ant-sized step of progress with the Carpenter Ants. I'd had a relatively collegial history with them, ever since my special CA pal Ant-thony helped me escape police custody. And they were the first types I managed to get through to—eventually.

You see, even with the EMP's "translation" of my thoughts into ant-speak (technically, ant-smell), there was still the challenge of, well, my thoughts.

To really get through to ants, Hope and Hank had taught me that you have to maintain this extreme, almost meditative level of focus on precisely what you want to say to them.

Easier said than thought! I couldn't even "ask" them to move a sugar cube into my cup of tea. Apparently, my brain was jumping around all over the place. And that's why, rather than simply sweeten my beverage, they followed my brain's lead and marched all over the place, too.

Was I ever going to connect with this different species? Was I going to fail at this? Was I truly useless and unemployable by anyone, and therefore incapable of ever getting to see Cassie again?

Fortunately, Hope got to the heart of my problem.

She helped me figure out that I couldn't focus because ultimately I kept thinking about Cassie. So, like the martial-arts master she is, Hope showed me how to turn that from a weakness into a strength: to use that burning concern as a laser beam to focus my intentions, and block out everything else.

Long story short, soon the Carpenters and I were on the same page, working together on an actual real-world training mission. We were supposed to retrieve the prototype of a signal decoy from one of Howard Stark's old storage facilities—which, unknown to Hank, was now the site of Avengers Compound. A fact that revealed itself to me rather clearly when Falcon almost pounded me into proto-hero-pulp.

Hank made an Ant-Cam, supposedly for "mission review and optimization." But I think he just wanted to teach his ants photography. Turns out one of those little guys is pretty good! We call him Ant-sel Adams.

Despite this, the CAs and I were of one mind enough for Ant-thony & co. to fly me out of there, with the prototype successfully in hand.

But there's a big difference between hitching rides from one kind of ant and performing multiple other tasks with multiple other types of ants. To carry off the Big Job, I'd have to learn to lead a variety of ants as a team.

That was what Hank and Hope had in mind when they brought me to the Hill.

The Hill was a big anthill in a part of Hank's backyard I'd not seen before, sort of a "community center" for all kinds of ants. I was to walk in there and become one with all of them. Or at least not get thrown out, devoured, or "panic-enlarge" my way out. Again.

I gamely climbed up to the top of the Hill, stuck my head into the entrance, and asked, "Who's ready for an *ant party?*"

If this weren't a group of ants, I'd describe the response as "crickets."

So I decided to change tack and let my hands do the talking: helping them out in their daily tasks. I started digging a tunnel. *Brilliant*, I thought! *Now they'll be able to easily transport themselves from—*

And then my sad, human attempt at a tunnel collapsed on me.

No worries! I switched strategies again. I looked around to see what the ants were actually *doing*, so I could join in on that. I spotted a group of them moving eggs and larvae from one side of the mound to the other. Apparently, they were moving their little ones to the warmer part of the mound, the area more exposed to heat from the sun. So that's how I'd help! I'd demonstrate my loyalty to the colony by helping care for their little, precious . . .

. . . Oh man, they did *not* take well to what must have looked like a strange "spaceman thing" touching their babies! Within seconds, I was swarmed.

Kudos to Scott, though; this swarming, I kept my size . . . and even better, kept my cool. I quickly barked orders: "Get away! Back off!" Which—being focused and clear instructions—the ants obeyed. Exactly like Hope had said.

But again, "getting ants to leave you alone" wasn't exactly the level of teamwork I was striving for.

So I pulled another trick out of my minuscule sleeve. I had brought some grains of sugar, to use for what entomologists technically refer to as "a bribe." I produced a few grains, and it worked!

But post–sugar consumption, they immediately blew me off again.

I climbed out of the mound, dejected and feeling like a failure. Definitely letting that mind of mine wander again, back to all the usual places. *Hank is going to send me back to jail. Hope will never love me. I'll never get to see Cassie again!*

When I walked back into the lab, full-sized again, Hank as always had the perfect words for my current state of mind: "What the hell are you doing here?"

Fortunately, Hope was a little more sympathetic. Even though she still had her doubts about me, she also reminded her dad of how his early experiments with the EMP were huge fails. How he almost got killed by an army of Bullet Ants, and only the threat of a common enemy (a very nasty centipede) won them over to his side.

She counseled me on how to present myself as more than just not a threat—as someone who they willingly followed because I "got them." Ants, just like people, respond better to direction from someone capable of seeing their perspective.

I hit the shrink button again and climbed back into the Hill, pondering Hope's challenge.

I had to find a way to rally the ants together, as one team aligned with me. But all of this felt like a huge asymmetry of power: me—the creature with the superior brain—using that brain to completely dominate a group of tiny beings and divert them from the essential tasks they had to undertake round the clock to preserve their colony.

In the back of my head, I felt like I could almost hear a voice, this time from the ants to me, saying: *Yes, you can get us to do things for you. But what have you ever done for us?*

It was a darn good question.

Sure, I'd barreled in there the first time and tried *my* idea of what would be useful to ants. You saw how that turned out.

So I took a tally: I knew what didn't work with them. I knew how to get them to follow orders. But there was still some key piece of connection missing, if I was to convince the little guys to carry out this high-wire mission. What was it?

Then it hit me.

I don't mean a great idea. No, what hit me was a wet, sticky drop from above. Then another.

The ants noticed it, too, or to be more precise, they smelled it. And they definitely did not like what they were smelling. They started backing away, even though the drops were dripping right onto their precious pile of sugar.

What was dripping into the anthill that was bothering the ants enough to make them avoid sugar?

I retracted my mask and got a whiff of what they were smelling: lemon juice.

It was dripping right onto the sugar pile, dissolving it into a disgusting, liquidy mess. A substance I had long despised in its typical aboveground form: "lemonade."

But to ants, lemon juice is toxic.

I poked my head up through the mound entrance to find a rotten lemon had somehow fallen on top of the anthill, most likely nudged by a squirrel seeking better foraging. It was mottled brown and mushy. And in addition to crushing the anthill, it was dripping poison into the ants' home.

And, even worse, it was way too big for even all those mighty Carpenter Ants to transport. Insensitive to pain, so not an easy target for the Bullet Ants. And no amount of insanity (or electricity) from the Crazy Ants would do the trick.

But I realized that now, for the first time, all of us—different ants and ant-sized human—had something precious: *a common enemy*. Just like Hank and the Bullet Ants vs. the centipede. A common cause where I could show that I was on their level.

I snapped into focus, issuing clear, simple directives: "Up! Out of the hole! Push the big yellow thing! Roll it. Roll it!"

Now I don't claim to be able to read an ant's facial expressions. But I swear I could see something shift in how they were looking at me. The ants noticed my focus on, and command of, the situation, and it registered. They saw how seriously I was taking this threat—as if it was equally a threat to me. That was the kind of reciprocity we'd need for them to take on the dangerous mission that loomed for me (and a few more of my fellow humans).

I know that because now, unlike in my first forays, they were looking to me, awaiting further instruction. They trusted me to lead them out of this.

The only problem was, despite our stellar teamwork, that lemon corpse just didn't want to roll. Did I mention the mushy part? Eventually it became clear that this wasn't going to work, no matter how many ants and I got behind it. The anthill was swiftly becoming unusable—and potentially lethal. The lemon-sugar mess was puddling dangerously close to the larvae. Finally, in desperation, I threw my armor-protected body between the yellow poison and their babies.

And then, the strangest thing happened. The ants swarmed me, once again.

But this time not to attack me. To lift me up. Back to my feet. Then they formed a kind of makeshift pyramid, or as I soon realized, the pointy tip of an arrow. Pointing up.

Now it was the ants speaking my language, being focused and direct with me: You. Up.

Tall.

And so finally, it felt like the right time to exercise my human dominance the right way—on *behalf of my team.*

Before you could say "thorax," I had boosted myself back up to human size, punting that horrible yellow stink bomb out of Hank's yard and into . . . well, it doesn't matter where. Then I shrank down once more to help the ants bury the noxious fluids it left behind and rebuild their home. Help that, this time around, they trusted me to render.

I learned more about leadership that day in an anthill than any MBA program could teach: observe your team, learn the correct leadership style for them, be clear and direct, and show that you understand where they're coming from.

It felt good. But do you know what really felt good? Knowing I could finally walk back into the lab, helmeted head held high, and tell a very surprised Hope and Hank that I—

Wait a minute! Was that my imagination, or did I see someone rushing into the house, as if to avoid me seeing him? Away from the lemon tree that, now that I looked at it, seemed suspiciously far away from the anthill. And was that lemon juice I smelled on Hank's hands later? He couldn't . . . he wouldn't . . . Or maybe that was a demonstration of how confident he was in me. Or at least his ants.

In any case, I counted myself satisfied with the day's work and shrank down to check in one last time with my tiny office.

And then, you know what words I finally managed to communicate to my team?

Ant party!!!

FAAMQ

Q: *How do you feel about being a human guinea pig for Hank Pym's experiments?*

A: I actually feel just fine about it! First of all, Hank and Janet used *themselves* as experimental fodder way before Hank started searching for nerdy thieves fresh out of prison. Also, although he can come off as a bit of a crank, I know Hank's main driving impulse is to help humanity. Just think of how rich he could have gotten from this tech by selling it to the highest bidder. But instead, he stuck to his principles and kept working on it until he had something that would benefit everyone. All of which means I know that he's not capable of designing something without also doing everything in his power to eliminate any harm to humans.

SUPER HEROING VS. PARENTING

THE ULTIMATE SMACKDOWN

I'VE DONE AND WILL do a lot of unexpected things in my life. But one thing's for certain: You're never going to catch a picture of me flashing a thumbs-up in my Ant-Man suit, saying one of those meme-ready blurbs like "Parents are the *real* Super Heroes."

Because, honestly, it's ridiculous to even compare the two occupations. It's not even apples vs. oranges; it's more like bowling balls vs. porcupines.

But I will admit: When you're ground down to exhaustion by either activity—Super Heroing or parenting—covered in any number of substances stinky and/or sticky, it is possible to mix them up.

So here's a handy guide to helping you figure out which incredibly noble and frequently thankless job you're currently undertaking.

	Super Hero	Parent
Origin Story	A strange encounter with an alien life-form or secret organization.	A very "Mai-Tai-forward" honeymoon.
Power-Up	An experimental military serum.	An experimental early morning blend of coffee and . . . more coffee.
Uniform	A high-tech flying mech suit.	Whichever hoodie smells least "ripe."
Secret Identity	Operative for a mysteriously acronymed government agency.	Often forgets actual name due to "parent brain."
Summons Allies By:	Yelling, "Assemble!"	Texting co-parent the emoji for "poop," "vomit," "house on fire," or all of the above.
Greatest Nemesis	A monster created from a cocktail of Super Soldier Serum and your own blood.	The undefeatable biological need for sleep.
Best Conflict-Ending Strategy	Turning villain's weapons against them.	"Who wants ice cream???"
Farthest Journey	The edge of the galaxy.	The only store that actually had a llama pinata.
Inspiring Mantra	Whatever it takes!	(whispered) "They're finally asleep."

	Super Hero	Parent
Must Avoid Detection By:	The media.	Judgy mother-in-law.
Most Reliable Defense	Vibranium armor.	Reading horror stories from parenting blogs.
Hail-Mary Move	Unveiling supernatural artifact.	Threatening to take away electronics.
Secret Vulnerability	Weak spot in armor joints.	Photos of the kids when they were little . . . and *asleep*.

CONCLUSION

So which job ultimately "takes the cape" as hardest? In my experience, hands down, it's parenting. Let me just put it this way: I have yet to have a bad guy throw up on me. On the beginning of a flight. A red-eye. Where we were sharing a single seat.

Go through that once, and you'll find yourself dreaming up gauntlets to take you to alternate timelines, too.

ANT-MAN & THE WASP:

SECOND DATE, OR SECOND CHANCE?

SOME COUPLES HAVE A "meet-cute." Some meet online. Many more meet at a bar than is really advisable.

Hope and I had a meet-*weird*.

And I don't mean just how, the first time we laid eyes on each other, I was waking up in her father's bed, surrounded by a brigade of sentry ants prepared to devour me like a giant bread crumb.

Or that we got to know each other's "vulnerabilities" through weeks of brutal martial-arts training. Or that the first time we shared a tear, it wasn't after an argument or a sappy movie. It was over the death of a half-inch-long insectile colleague named "Ant-thony." (RIP wherever you are, little guy!)

And the way we originally met . . . ? Let's just say, how many relationships have you had that began with you breaking into your (future) partner's dad's basement to steal a piece of secret technology?

At least there was one way in which our relationship was typical: We had a little "difficult patch" and broke up for a while. But even then, the way we got back together was . . . okay, once again, weird.

I want to share the story with you, because it kind of leads to later events with the Avengers. But one thing I've learned about being in a relationship (sometimes the hard way!) is that two different people can experience the same thing together . . . in two entirely different ways. So to make sure I'm getting the story straight, I'm sitting down with Hope to hear, and share, her take on what happened.

It all started right after our Pym Tech heist, when I was recruited by some Avengers to go fight some other Avengers. (See? It's not just couples who have break-ups.) Unfortunately, in doing so, I kind of borrowed the Ant-Man suit and took it to Germany without asking permission.

Hope has quite a different take on this. As she recounts it, "My father and I had *just* begun to trust you, and to think of you as someone who could possibly join the tight-knit circle of what we Pym/Van Dynes had devoted our lives to. In my mom's case, what she'd sacrificed so much of her life for. And besides trust, I was starting to develop some . . . non-professional feelings for you, too. And then you went and betrayed *everything*."

That perspective explains why Hope (and Hank) cut off all ties to me for the next two years while I was put under house arrest for acting as an "unregistered Super Hero" in that intra-Avenger fracas.

Still, you know me! I prefer to focus on the positive. Like Hope's and my emotional reunion when she came to spring me from house arrest to help her and Hank.

But as before, Hope says she experienced somewhat . . . different feelings during that reunion. In her words: "Disgust. Did you spend the entire two years in that bathrobe? And also, disgust on a deeper level. Seeing you again, remembering you in Dad's suit, and what you had done with it, it brought up all kinds of complicated feelings I'd been trying to put behind me."

Fortunately for both of us (and eventually, the world) Hope doesn't let any feeling get in the way of a mission. Especially one involving her mother. Janet Van Dyne, wife of Hank, formerly known as The Wasp, had been trapped in the Quantum Realm for decades, but she had recently found a way to contact us. And now we were going to try to find her by going back into Hank's Quantum Tunnel.

Except to do that, we needed a key component, and the only way we could get it was from this sleazebag underground tech dealer named Sonny Burch. So we set up a meeting with him to buy it. Only, during that meeting, Burch figured out who Hope was and double-crossed her to steal Hank's lab, which had been shrunk down to the size of a suitcase.

Hope, again, remembers this a bit differently. According to her, "There was no 'we.' It was me alone at that skeevy hotel bar with Burch and his cronies, then suddenly I was fighting them off alone, then you showed up too late, then you let that glowing woman named 'Ghost' run off with the lab!"

I'm not sure this is a completely fair assessment. But I can see why Hope felt that way, because at that point, she was still very untrusting of me. Our first meetup in two years, and the first thing I do is put her dad's life's work in jeopardy—for the second time.

Scott "glass half full of Pym Particles" here again: We got the suitcase lab back!

However, Hope reminds me, "Actually, before that, we got captured by Ghost—who was only going to let us go if we healed her quantum energy problems by *killing my mom!*"

Obviously, that was unacceptable, so we managed to escape, got the tunnel working again, and even, finally, got into direct communication with Janet Van Dyne. What a relief!

Again, though, from Hope's POV, "relief" wasn't what she was feeling. She reminds me that it wasn't exactly direct communication, as—thanks to a bizarre property of the Quantum Realm—Janet was actually speaking *through me.*

As she puts it, "Can you imagine *anything* more disturbing than hearing your long-thought-to-be-dead mother's words coming out of your ex-boyfriend's mouth?"

Honestly, I can't. And I'd really rather not try. But still, we'd actually found Janet! And now the only challenge was figuring out *how* we could get into the Quantum Realm to rescue her.

Here, too, Hope remembers a few more complications. "There was also the fact your prison buddies had ratted Dad and me out, getting us arrested by the FBI. Plus Ghost still had my dad's stolen work."

Of course, she's right, and that was a really rough road.

I don't mean to downplay it. I think it was just that, because Hope and I had survived tougher scrapes, my confidence in *us*—a confidence that I understand she wasn't quite feeling at that point—was keeping me going.

And this is where I'm really glad I asked Hope to join me for this, because what she says next is a bit of a revelation to me . . .

"Scott, you don't know what it was like growing up with Hank Pym as a father . . . seeing how important all of this was to him . . . feeling how he lived and died over every breakthrough and setback. And here we were, on the cusp of losing all of it."

She's right. I really had no clue about how deeply all this cut for her until now. Both Hope and Hank play things so close to the vest, sometimes it's hard to see how hard the disappointments hurt them where it counts.

But to get back to the story, I definitely owed Hank Pym a "Get Out of Jail Free" card, so I used some of my old ex-con skills to bust us out of FBI custody. Then we took on Ghost, endured a seemingly endless series of car chases, and battled back and forth for possession of that shrunken lab all the way to San Francisco Bay. That's where I used the suit to go giant and snatch Hank's lab back once and for all.

As I talked about briefly before, using Pym Particles to

turn gigantic takes a toll. Although I successfully grabbed the (then, to me, minuscule) lab, I also lost consciousness and plunged into the bay—where the World's Greatest Super Hero rescued me from a watery grave.

Hope seems okay with this description.

Then, after a tiny-hair-raising expedition into the Quantum Realm, Hank managed to get Janet back out. Whew! All's well that ends well.

Right?

At this point, Hope remains silent for a minute. Then, slowly and carefully, she speaks. "I spent that day in absolute terror about my mom."

She continues, "And that was on top of all the tough stuff we'd been through. Someone always going to prison. Multiple sociopaths trying to kill us, sometimes at the same time. And then, having my mom come back from what we thought was the dead after three decades? I know I act like nothing fazes me, but it was *a lot*."

She's right. It was. And here's what I'm telling Hope, and what I also want to tell you, about whatever you're going through—on the inside or outside. Whether it involves glowing quantum ladies or not:

You don't have to deal with this alone.

In a strange way, I think that insight might be part of how Hope and I eventually managed to patch things up. I had broken her and her Dad's trust, massively. But during all this we found a way of connecting again.

You see, Hope didn't share a lot of what she was going through at the time. In fact, I'm just finding out about a lot of it right now, as I write this!

But as the two of us dove back into the fray together, part of me was working twice as hard to show her how dedicated I was to her and her dad (and mom)—to prove how much they meant to me. I'd like to think that just enough of that "being there 200 percent" got through to her.

And since I don't see Hope shaking her head "No," I'll keep going and conclude with one more thought:

"Being there 200 percent" is something we all can do for each other, no matter what kind of relationship we're in. Or what relationship we're trying to mend. I managed to prove to Hope that she wasn't alone, because I was there—and not going anywhere.

And on this point, Hope says our stories are in perfect alignment.

FAAMQ

Q: *Aren't you worried that this technology could fall into the wrong hands?*

A: Um, *yeah.* Something like 95 percent of the stuff I get wrapped up in involves "technology falling into the wrong hands." To say nothing of the risks of the technology even in the *right* hands. Even with less advanced tech, this is always a risk. But what's the alternative? Don't continue innovating?

The way my fellow Super Heroes and I try to address this issue is by keeping a close eye on what we call "a change in the battlefield." By that I mean we pay attention to the news and take note when something that's been basically impossible for a human to achieve suddenly happens. Then we know there's been a "battlefield change," that some new ability or device has entered the arsenal of Earth dwellers (or visitors). And that it's probably not going to be used for good.

SIDE BY SIDE

SUPER HEROING WITH YOUR SIGNIFICANT OTHER

OKAY, SO NOW HOPE and I were back together, for what seemed like the long haul. Which meant we were now facing one of those paradoxes of life: Sometimes you fight the most with the one you love. But what if you're also simultaneously fighting Super Villains?

Clearly disregarding the time-tested maxim "Don't date at work," I've come to appreciate both the perks and pitfalls of this lifestyle.

Confusingly, though, those perks and pitfalls often go hand in hand. To illustrate what I mean, imagine working, very closely and on a daily basis, with the person you're most attracted to in the world. And then, during that work, seeing them at their very best: strong, steady, steely under even the most terrifying conditions. Always cool-headed and mission-focused. And to top it all off, bringing all those qualities to the service (and usually, life-saving) of others!

Sometimes it takes more than Super Hero strength to *not* feel overwhelmed by a gusher of love and admiration.

And when you do find yourself with them in a moment of respite, especially if it happens to be in a beautiful location (hey, Super Villains like to get outside sometimes, too), it can get very confusing. Part of your brain is screaming, "Remember why you two are here together," while another part is murmuring, "Hey, couldn't we just steal a moment to enjoy this nice place we ended up together?"

To say nothing of those situations when you're trapped with them in a very small space and are reminded of *just how darn good she always smells.*

And that's one of the good problems!

A larger complication in this perpetually unbalanced work-life balance is what I call *fighting other battles.* Perhaps this rings true in your relationships as well? You're yelling and screaming at each other over the stupidest thing, and often it's not until later that you realize that all that rage was not even truly about *that* thing! It was about a completely *different* stupid thing that you were annoyed about earlier, but which never got resolved.

The dangerous part is when that pent-up unfought fight spills over into the actual life-or-death one you're currently engaged in. "Oh, so you can aim that reducing disc right at an oncoming military transport vehicle, but you can't toss a T-shirt into the laundry hamper?" "Oh, so you'll take three punches to the head from a mercenary but you're afraid to try one bite of my world-famous 'Chili Dog Meatloaf'?"

The good news is, there's a quick way out of any of these intertwined battles. It's by reciting a set of words so devastatingly powerful, even Doctor Strange has nothing that competes.

Those magical words? "You're right, I'm sorry."

Another anxiety I've felt in all my relationships, but which takes on a sharper hue on the battlefield, is one I call *exposing your true self*. And I don't mean that alter-ego/secret identity game. Let's face it: Ever since Tony Stark straight-up announced to the world, "I am Iron Man!" that whole move has lost its subversive cool factor. Nowadays, the only reaction I get from clearing my throat, retracting my helmet, and proclaiming in a deep, rich, dramatic baritone, "*I am Ant-Man*," is, "Noted. And would Ant-Man like curly fries with that?"

No, what I'm talking about is revealing your worst traits to the last person you'd ever want to think any less of you.

For me, that worry comes up around the issue of showing fear around Hope. Which I *know*, on an intellectual level, is just silly. Maybe it's a hero complex (yes, even actual heroes get them). But for me at least it's real, and it's a constant struggle.

And what's odd is, it's not really even my biggest problem. I'm fairly proud of the fact that—whether facing down one half of Earth's Mightiest Heroes or the Universe's Biggest Threat—I don't scare that easily. But Hope doesn't even seem *capable of fear*. It's like the woman was born without an amygdala. Or maybe she's just trained it out of herself, with that same steely drive and determination that first made her a hero and now has made her a business leader.

Either way, the upshot is, when I get even just a little bit scared, I get more scared of Hope *seeing me scared*. If that was confusing to follow, imagine trying to keep a handle on it in the middle of a fight.

Sometimes in the heat of battle, I can't help but stop and think, "*She* likes *me*?" This usually happens right before I get knocked unconscious.

Another challenge to my sense of combat-time couple zen is *temper*. When all your senses are locked onto defeating your foe, you don't have a lot of mental gas left in the tank to choose your words carefully. So what happens when the two of you have a plan, but it's swiftly going wrong? Or even worse, when the plan is still good but one of you forgot or screwed up their part? And the bad guy is using that advantage to close in!

There was this one time when the two of us were cut off from our resizing controls, a set of mechanical gears were getting ready to chew us up, and Hope felt, correctly, that we could have escaped the situation more easily had I loaded in the magnetized grappling hook rather than the unmagnetized one.

However, Hope chose to express this sentiment in language so . . . colorful, it informed me that she did indeed know a four-letter word besides "can't."

Now, in even the most benign situations, the tendency in a couple is to lash out, because you know the other person can "take it." You feel, as it were, safe.

But in battle, you're literally the opposite of safe.

And you know that expression "Watch out or you might say something you regret"? In the civilian world, that's of course great advice, along with "Never go to bed angry." You really do never know with 100 percent certainty if you might never see a loved one alive again. But for romantically connected Super Heroes, there's a very high statistical chance this is the very last thing you ever say to them!

Long story short, Hope and I obviously survived that

near–metal mastication, as did our relationship. It just takes some getting used to, that idea that you have to fight to preserve both at the same time.

Another layer to that self-consciousness, which might be unique to me but I suspect really isn't, is the additional meta-fear of *letting her dad down*. Nowadays I think I've proven myself to Hank Pym as a proper heir to the Ant-Man suit. But in a funny way, having earned his approval, now I feel even more anxious about losing even a drop of it. Maybe because it was so hard-won, or maybe because I'm starting to see him as a model for the kind of hero I want to be.

Now obviously, Hope is in every possible way her own person who makes her own decisions. But somehow, subconsciously, there's still a part of me that feels like I'm living on borrowed time. Like one day, I'm going to screw things up too much, and Hank is going to swoop in (likely ferried by a river of ants) and say, "Nope. This phase of the 'experiment' is over."

So that, along with the other stuff, translates into a kind of perfectionism I try to hold myself to all the time, which is completely unrealistic. And completely impossible to remove from the ongoing soundtrack of "You don't really deserve this, Scott" that lives in my brain 24/7. Even though I've bounced back countless times, there's still a live, burning piece of me that sees myself as no more than convict/divorcé/absentee dad. It takes more mental energy than I'd like to quiet that voice, or at least convince it that others don't see me that way. And when things sometimes go south with Hope, as they do in all relationships, I can hear it shouting, "You see? She knows you're still no good at the core."

It also doesn't help when I remember how happy my ex Maggie is with her new guy. That accusatory brain voice now switches over and starts asking, "Are you just standing in the way of Hope being much happier with another guy?"

Now the good news is, having lived and loved through this rocky terrain, I've found some bright spots as well. One is that Hope and I—like most couples who've been together for a while—have a *secret language*. Shorthand, absurd nicknames, shared references, and inside jokes that can be as helpful in situations with no time to spare as it is annoying when we play Charades with friends. Cracking those jokes can also be critical to boosting each other's morale in moments when all seems lost. On the other hand, an inopportune but uncontrollable snicker can also be the thing that fatally gives away your position.

Along these lines, we've also developed a pretty keen

talent for *anticipating the other's moves*. No, not the way you're undoubtedly thinking—on the dance floor. There's no hope for me there. But when we're locked in combat, even a telepath couldn't keep up with the speed of our nonverbal communication.

And as unbelievable as it sounds, taking on evil can be a really helpful form of *relationship building*. Love experts say that for a couple to stand the test of time, they should have an "indoor hobby" and an "outdoor hobby." Fortunately, when you're going on high-stakes missions, you often get both of those things in one afternoon.

Heroing it up together also helps with your sense of *relationship chill*. Put simply, after a long day or week or quantum half-decade of battling baddies, the two of us just come home and collapse on the sofa. Which is heaven. We get to do normal couple things, like disagree over who's killing the plants faster. Hope gets to let her guard down and get extremely, almost frighteningly passionate over who *needs* to go home from *Dating-Show Island*. I get to see her actually, atypically, be *bad* at something. (For example: When we play a video game together . . . well, let's just say that Hope would probably be better mowing down zombies in real life—not like that would ever happen!)

But the main saving grace is, we're just too exhausted to argue about *anything*. Which I admit doesn't help with the "unresolved issues" point I made above. But it's a nice feeling to come home and settle into. It makes our humble, slightly stained sofa feel more secure than even the Raft prison.

And that feeling is just one example of how what Hope and I do together helps us *appreciate couplehood*. There are *soooo* many "troubled loners" in our profession, on both the good and evil side, it almost seems like a job requirement.

By contrast, Hope and I balance each other. She's calm, I'm alert. She's sky, I'm earth. She commands, I obey.

But all these perks of being "heroes with benefits" pale next to the biggest one of all. The greatest advantage to being lovers *and* fighters is that it gives you a true sense of *life's priorities*. A lot of the time we Super Heroes don't exactly see the people we're saving; we have to just hold the idea in our heads, abstractly. In our case, we see what's at stake every moment, and then Hope races me into the house, wins (of course), flashes me that incredibly hard-won half smile, and a light in my heart comes on and recharges all my batteries at once.

Put simply, every day the two of us come back home

together, in one piece, is a miracle, a precious gift. *The most precious gift*, to which no super-power granted by serum or gamma ray or technology could compare.

And when you've got that, you are the most literal definition of invincible.

FAAMQ

Q. *What's your favorite thing to grow or shrink for fun?*

A. Let me be clear up front: Pym Particles are *not* to be used for fun—they are serious business. But *hypothetically*, I imagine it would be pretty fun—and only a little sticky—to have your kid walk downstairs on a Saturday morning and find a giant jelly donut waiting for them. Especially if you were, say, hypothetically trapped in your house for two years and racking your brain for new things to keep that hypothetical kid happy.

Man, I miss those hypothetical days.

INFINITY SAGA: ABRIDGED

DO YOU GUYS REMEMBER when something really bizarre happened to the world for five years? Well, technically, half of you remember it, while the other half of you might not because you literally stopped existing.

Well, there were a *lot* of explanations floating around, during and after, as to how that all happened. But there's only one actual, accurate one. And even though I myself was near-invisibly tiny and trapped in a quantum machine in the back of a van at the time, I got the official scoop later, from the Avengers who were there.

So since I've gotten the story filled in for me, I thought I should share it with you. In other words, you're getting it straight from the source . . . that was standing right *next* to the source.

I had just crawled out of Hank Pym's Quantum Tunnel into a world in which, apparently, five years had passed, and billions of people were suddenly gone. And once I eventually stopped hyperventilating, and found Cassie alive and well and *so much bigger*, I did the next logical thing.

I went to the Avengers.

I mean, the Avengers who were still around.

Coming to Avengers Compound was . . . well, "bittersweet" doesn't begin to capture the assortment of emotions surging through me.

All of which were only stirred up further by what I saw in Cap and Natasha when I'd babbled enough into the security camera for them to finally let me in. These were two people I'd thought were born with stoic expressions, but now even they couldn't hide the slight mouth quivers, the pain etched into their faces, the hollowness behind their eyes.

At first, we just embraced, in silence. Silence seemed

like the only possible place to start, before we could broach the unspeakable.

Now of course Cassie had told me what she understood had happened to the world, but her civilian's-eye view only gave me a fraction of the big picture. I needed to know so much more.

Nat began.

"You know about the Infinity Stones, right?"

"Yes," I responded. "Five stones of extraordinary power."

"Six." Nat frowned, but continued. "So for some time, Thanos has been gathering them all, because whoever has all six in their possession can do enormous damage to the universe."

"Which explains the . . . missing people?"

Cap interjected, his rage uncharacteristically getting the better of him, "That maniac took out half of all life. Not just on Earth. In the *universe*."

Nat explained, "Thanos apparently decided that the universe can't support so much life, so he was going to cull the whole thing down to size."

Now shock and disbelief were vying for attention in my brain. "So, he . . . actually managed to get all six Stones?"

Cap nodded and resumed the tale. "From everywhere.

He beat down Thor and the Hulk to get one. He even somehow got one from Doctor Strange!" (We now know it was all part of Strange's plan, but at this moment, I could see it baffled and frustrated Cap to recount it.)

"It gets even worse," said Nat. "What he was willing to do to get them. He killed most of the Asgardians who'd just barely escaped Ragnarok. He tortured one daughter and sacrificed another. He ripped the Mind Stone right out of Vision's forehead. Fatally."

"Wow," I responded, again in disbelief. But really, how else to react? To be candid, I barely knew Vision, or any of the other victims she described. But still. Wow.

"We tried to stop Thanos," added Cap. "We made a massive last stand in Wakanda. An incredible effort, even by our standards. Managed to pick off some of his generals. But we didn't . . ."

And here Cap paused, and gave a sigh that seemed to contain so much more hurt than one man could ever let out.

Nat's eyes were welling up—almost as much a shock as anything they were telling me—as she finished Cap's thought. "We fought as hard as we possibly could, as hard as *anyone* could. And it still wasn't enough! We lost so many. *So many*, even before the Snap! We—"

"Sorry, the . . . what?"

Cap picked up the thread again. "Once he obtained the Mind Stone, Thanos gathered all six into a custom-made gauntlet, this special glove that controls them. And then, with all the destructive forces of the universe combined into one place, he just did . . . *this*."

Cap snapped his fingers. Another moment of silence. By now I was getting used to these. Silence seemed to be the only way to get through all this. But I had to hear this to the end.

"He . . . snapped his fingers? And everyone just went away?"

"Half of everyone, but yeah," Nat answered. "And we've spent the past five years trying to figure out the what, how, and what-the-hell-do-we-do-now."

Another of those impossible-to-form questions arose: "How are . . . I mean, how is everyone . . . everyone who's still . . . ?"

"Thor and Banner both took it pretty hard," said Cap. "We haven't been in contact, but we know Tony has visited Bruce a few times down in Mexico. Thor, we know he made it—but no one's seen him since. Last I heard he was holed up in New Asgard."

I didn't have to ask how Nat and Cap were. It was radiating from their every pore.

So now, after another few moments of quiet, just

sitting with all this, something began to itch in my brain.

Something that felt like an infinitesimal, almost quark-sized, particle of hope.

My "rational" brain—which was currently being flooded by the emotional part after all I'd seen that day and heard from my friends—tried to quell the itch. Told it to go away and stop being silly.

But if there's one takeaway from my highly unusual life, it's that sometimes the tiniest things can offer the key to salvation.

So I couldn't *quite* silence the itch. Nor could I find the words or thoughts to scratch it. Instead, it started to slowly balloon inside me. And make me very uncomfortable—but not necessarily in a bad way . . .

I began to pace. Like *really* pace, hard. Cap seemed almost concerned I was going to damage the Avengers Compound floor and asked, "Scott. Are you okay?"

Finally, I couldn't keep the itch inside anymore, or it would destroy me. So I dared to voice my crazy inner hunch aloud.

"Have either of you ever studied quantum physics?"

"Only to make conversation," Natasha replied.

So I told them. What had happened to me when I was trapped in the Quantum Realm. How time seemed to work differently there. How five years in the real world had seemed like only five hours for me.

And as I was describing this, I began sharing that itch, that spark—how I thought my experience in the Quantum Realm meant that maybe, just maybe, we could use what I learned there to resolve this.

Could we somehow fix what Thanos had done and control the chaos by accessing the Quantum Realm—and even more incredibly, channeling its strange powers?

And before I knew it, the three of us had hatched a plan . . . sort of. The very haziest of plans, really. But just enough of a plan to take to Tony Stark, so he could smash it back into atoms and rebuild it as an actual plan.

But it was still, even by Ant-Man and Avengers standards, the very craziest of plans.

And the craziest part of it by far? That a guy who couldn't keep a job scooping ice cream could maybe save the entire universe.

FROM BEGINNING TO ENDGAME

IF YOU'VE GOTTEN THIS far in the book, you've heard me answer a few questions. But here's one that I'm going to need quite a few pages for.

Hey Scott, you were an active participant in the most epic event to ever happen to Earth. WHAT HAPPENED???

Okay, so as I was just recounting last chapter, I wasn't actually around for the Blip myself. But I got filled in on what had happened by Nat and Cap. And now our next move was to go crash Tony Stark's cabin in the woods with my idea for fixing things: using the Quantum Realm to bring everyone back.

When we first pulled into Tony's place, just like when I first made it back to Avengers Compound from my Blip van-trap, I was a grab bag of emotions. On the one hand, I was still processing the overwhelming grief that for everyone else had become part of the texture of everyday life. On the other hand, there was the idea that I—the one Avenger who had missed the chance to stop Thanos—might get another chance at that now. That little old me could, somehow, fix . . . *all of this*?

Then again, what if it didn't work? What if I unleashed the cruelty of getting everyone's hopes up in an already unbearable time, only to squash them for good? What if I failed the Avengers—and Hope?

But I had to mentally shelve all that and just keep my stomach from boiling over with a jangly combo of nerves and anticipation. Because I was about to pitch my idea—a notion from way outside the bounds of contemporary science, and which I'd spent, at most, a day thinking about—to one of the world's greatest geniuses.

I don't want to get ahead of myself, but considering what happened later on, I will always treasure this one moment of trying to solve an overwhelming problem right alongside the great Tony Stark.

Unfortunately, he wasn't buying it.

Tony started raising objections, mentioning some things which I sort-of-but-not-completely remembered from college: the Planck Scale, the Deutsch Proposition. I can't say I fully understood his argument. But I knew that it came down to, essentially, no. It'll never work.

Which is not usually the kind of reasoning that stops a guy like Tony. But in this case, it was a deal breaker. And I think I know why.

As we sat there, with Tony and his young daughter, Morgan, I could see how head-over-heels Tony was for that adorable little girl. Let's just say there was something way more potent than a mini Arc Reactor powering his heart.

So while his mouth spoke of pasts and futures, I know Tony's mind was unshakably tied to the present. I could imagine what he was thinking: *Jumping to and from multiple timelines is literally uncharted territory. Which means uncharted risks. Among those risks: losing the light and center of my life.* I made a final emotional plea to Tony: "I know you have a lot on the line. You have a wife, a daughter. But I lost someone . . . very important to me. A lot of people did. And now—now we have a chance to bring her back, to bring everyone back, and you're telling me that you won't even—"

Tony interrupted, "That's right, Scott: I won't even. I can't."

Well, what could I say to that? I remembered with blindingly painful clarity those days in prison, just *dreaming* of getting to bounce my little bundle of Cassie on my knee. Reflecting, over and over, that my own decisions had snatched that precious, once-in-a-lifetime sweetness away. And here I was, effectively proposing that exact path to Tony.

I couldn't even imagine what I would do if faced with the choice of saving the universe or saving my Cassie.

Moments later, Cap, Nat, and I were headed back to the car, empty-handed. There was nothing left to say. Tony had saved so many lives. Now he just wanted a chance to have a life of his own.

So we left his place to hit up our next really big brain, Bruce Banner. But here's where things got weird. Well, weird*er*. There was no more Bruce vs. Hulk. Now he'd put it all together into one cool-headed, giant-headed, smart-strong guy.

The best part, though, was that Bruce actually liked my idea! And soon we were giving Quantum-Tunnel-traveling the old "test drive." Only thing is . . . we didn't quite get it off the ground.

But fortunately, that's when Tony walked in.

He'd had a change of heart. Which, if you know how complicated his heart is, is a huge deal.

A little after that, a raccoon from space showed up. I don't think he knew my name. I was just happy to meet a raccoon who could talk.

But soon enough, Tony got the whole directed-Quantum-Tunnel-travel mechanism to work! And once Clint performed the first test *without* coming back as a baby or a geezer (unlike me, as I'll detail in the next chapter), we knew we had solved the equation! Now it was time to hash out the plan.

The idea was, we would identify specific, recent points on alternate timelines where we knew an Infinity Stone to be. And then we'd use the Quantum Tunnel to "jump" to that timeline and grab the stone there. Once in possession of all six, we would have the same power Thanos used to create the Blip—except we'd use that power to bring everyone back.

So, with our team of intergalactic allies assembled, we had to figure out the biggest jewel heist in history. We broke into separate teams: Thor and Rocket were going to Asgard—Old Asgard, I mean. The one in space. Clint and Natasha were going to a planet named Vormir, also in space. Nebula and Rhodey were off to the definitely-in-space planet Morag. As for me,

I was headed to exotic, faraway . . . New York City.

I'm not going to lie—I was a little disappointed that seemingly everybody *but* me was getting to go to space. But in a way, space was coming to all of us, right here.

You see, until then I knew about as little as my fellow civilians about all the mind-boggling varieties of extra-terrestrials in the universe. I mean, I've been in the Quantum Realm, which is full of all *kinds* of crazy stuff, but I can state with almost 100 percent certainty that the Quantum Realm doesn't include *intelligent life-forms*.

And yes, sure, we all hypothesized that "something else was out there" when a hammer-wielding god showed up from beyond. Suspicions may have been raised further when an army of those ugly Chitauri and their even uglier Leviathan robo-lizard transports rained down onto New York City.

But to me and the average person just going about their life *without* regular galactic dispatches from Captain Marvel, it might have well looked like that was basically a one-time hole in the NY skyline that got patched up.

And speaking of New York, that's where Tony, Cap, Bruce, and I were headed for our part of the heist. Apparently three of the six Stones could be obtained in an alternate version of New York City in 2012.

See? You really can get almost anything in NYC.

So the four of us set off through the Quantum Tunnel and arrived during the legendary Battle of New York of 2012, when the Avengers had protected the Earth from those interdimensional creeps. And now, unlike in our 2012, I was kind of taking part in the fight! Or at least, like, I was *right next* to it.

But traveling to this battle was only the first step. Once we were there, we had to figure out how to actually nab the Mind Stone and Space Stone—without being discovered, captured, and killed. A near-impossible task, right?

Well, you forget who I was working with!

My job was to get tiny (check!), sneak into the Space Stone–carrying Tony Stark's custom-made artificial heart (check . . .) and disable it to give him a heart attack (check?). All without a manual!

In the end, I pulled it off. Enough. I managed to do just the right amount of damage to give other-timeline Iron Man a "mild cardiac dysrhythmia"—as my time's Iron Man had requested—and thereby create a distraction.

Unfortunately, once my Tony grabbed the Tesseract case, the Hulk emerged from the stairwell and knocked Tony down. But not *my* Hulk, the *other* Hulk. The one from 2012 . . . but, like, an alternate 2012. You know what, let's call him "Alt-2012 Hulk."

Alt-2012 Hulk knocked Tony over, the case slid across

the floor, and in the end all my distraction did was allow Alt-2012 Loki to escape with the Space Stone. One can only imagine what *that* led to.

That's when I uttered a phrase that may as well describe my entire life:

"That wasn't supposed to happen, was it?"

Tony and Cap and I regrouped in a freshly smashed car, and this time the pain of recollection cuts deeper. I remember all too well how I laid into Tony, accusing him of never being on board with this plan (maybe with a little of my own anger at his rejection of my original pitch) and of "ruining the Time Heist." I wailed and wailed about how we'd lost our one shot at this, and how there were "no do-overs."

Talk about something Scott Lang of all people should have known better than to say! If there was anything I wish I could do over, it was that conversation.

Fortunately, at that moment Tony and Cap made the wise decision to stop listening to me. Instead, they cobbled together another, even wilder plan to timeline-hop their way into obtaining enough Pym Particles, from a timeline in the 1970s they'd never even experienced, to take *another* shot at that Space Stone. The shot I had ruled out as impossible.

Then they made the even wiser decision to give me

a job more suitable to my pay grade: take the scepter containing the Mind Stone back to the Compound. Scott Lang: Super Schlepper.

But you know what? They were spot-on for that moment. It's called leadership, folks.

Fortunately, plan "Disco Timeline" worked. So soon we had all six Stones and, thanks to Tony, a replacement gauntlet to put them in. Bruce, as the most gamma-irradiated among us, volunteered, and gave his fingers a much, much more positively inclined snap.

And then, something weird happened. In the sky. I saw birds.

But that's not the weird thing.

What was weird was, suddenly there were way more birds than before. You might even say probably *twice* as many. But somehow, strangely, that instantaneous explosion of life filled me with a tiny feeling of optimism I couldn't even remember experiencing, because it had been so long.

It turned out to be a very short-lived feeling. Because then those birds were joined by another, very unwelcome flock of beings in the sky: Thanos and his army.

Within nanoseconds, Avengers Compound was under massive air attack from Thanos and his fleet. With a skeleton crew, zero advance warning, and no security protocols in place, we Avengers were sitting ducks.

A distress call screamed out of my wrist-com. It was Rhodey. He said he, Bruce, and Rocket were trapped in the rubble on a lower level. Surrounded by rapidly rising floodwaters!

I shrunk down, slipped my way through the labyrinth of rubble and wreckage, and found my way to the three of them. Then I did a funky little trick to shield them safely inside my hand while simultaneously growing gigantic enough to burst us all out of that disaster zone.

So there we there, the four of us, safely back above-ground, the three of them safely in my giant hand. I'm not proud to admit this, but I enjoyed the fact that, for just one brief moment, the Hulk was like my little plaything.

But that moment passed quickly. For below me I saw a wartime assemblage taking place before my eyes, like no other that has ever been or probably ever will be.

On one side, glistening black, armored demonic creatures of varying shapes and forms, spilling onto our planet from an even more terrifyingly repulsive spacecraft.

On the other, an endless, relentless flood of good. Heroes of every color, size, species. Every hero I could think of, and many I couldn't have even imagined. All with one heart, one goal, one stand they had lived their entire lives to take. Now.

And . . . could it be? My giant heart skipped a beat at the sight of a very familiar pair of mechanized wings.

Wasp wings.

Our second snap had brought back billions. And yet at this moment, it took only one of them for me to finally feel like *my* world had come back. Hope and *hope* together, a sight so beautiful it seemed to gleam straight into my tinted helmet.

Then we all heard it. The tiny but somehow audible-to-thousands command of Captain America:

Avengers . . . assemble!!!

Which was immediately followed by a much, much bigger noise: the battle cry of the mightiest beings in existence, fired together as if in a mighty forge of purpose. The pure joy of uniting all our muscles, brains, circuits, god powers, and *souls* hardened into one unstoppable spear point aimed right into the darkest heart in the universe.

And then we charged. They ran at us. Missiles, blades, bursts, and beams lit up the night, as both sides met in one existential, future-defining crunch.

One of those Leviathans, the size of a C-5, soared through the smoky air, threatening to disgorge even more baddies. But waiting for it was one Ant-Man, the size of a skyscraper, connecting with a right hook that sent it smashing, fatally, into the planet it had meant to conquer.

Then I put my massive feet to work, flattening one of Thanos's giant soldier-beasts the size of a rearing elephant.

I heard Clint over the comm channel asking what to do with the gauntlet, still pulsing with our indescribably hard-won Stones. Cap said to get them as far away as possible, but Bruce objected. "Far" wasn't good enough to keep the thing out of Thanos's hands. He could use it to destroy half of life. Again. We had to get the Stones we'd pilfered back to their original points in their original timelines . . . now!

Just one slight problem, noted Tony. The Quantum Tunnel—the conduit that had let us steal them in the first place—got pulverized in that opening salvo on Avengers Compound. There was no way to take them back.

Or *was there?*

I remembered the little Quantum Tunnel that had started it all: Hank's experimental one I'd been trapped in during the Blip. The one in my best friend Luis's van.

I clicked my key fob like the most desperate car owner ever in a parking garage designed by M. C. Escher. *Come on, Scott,* I chided myself, even after days of unbelievable following unbelievable, *there's no way that van could have survived the—*

I've never heard a sweeter sound in my life than the opening bars of "La Cucaracha" blaring somewhere from this plain full of fire and screams.

Valkyrie sighted that brown, four-wheeled box of salvation, somehow miraculously saved in the collapse of the Compound. Unfortunately, now it was being overrun by a pack of Thanos's canine-monster Outriders.

To Cap, though, that was just my next assignment. He told me to get the van tunnel working, and they'd get the Stones to me. I scanned the path from us to the van warily. One of those Outriders was enough to chomp through three Avengers for an appetizer. I saw dozens.

And then I felt a hand on my shoulder. Hope was by my side. As always. And suddenly the path felt completely clear.

We gave each other a look, and with one mind we went tiny, and we went for it. We darted through the battlefield and landed in the driver's seat—only to find a slight problem: The van's engine wouldn't start. Which meant no tunnel. And no escape from Thanos, ever. No matter how many timelines we braved.

Dear Reader, you know how two of my constant refrains have been "You never know where life will take you" and "*Why* did *I* have to go to prison?"

Let's just say, if I hadn't spent a good few years of

my life hanging out with cons, I wouldn't know how to hot-wire a vehicle.

But it took a few tries and more minutes than anyone had time for. While I fiddled, I saw through the windshield that crazy giant golden glove heading toward me in the most battle-ravaged way possible. Clint came under fire, and Black Panther took the gauntlet from him, parkouring over—and sometimes through—foe after foe. Thanos rushed toward him, only to be temporarily sandwiched between two of Wanda's red-hot-magic flying boulders. Black Panther almost got felled by a magic ground-tentacle, only to have Spider-Man swing by and pick up the ultimate baton.

By this time, I was still only getting grinding noises from the engine, but any second it might be that fateful "chunk" I needed to hear. In the meantime, I got a nice view of Wanda lifting and toasting Thanos redly, only to hear him bellow for his hench-creatures to "rain fire" on the whole battle, his own troops be damned.

I confess I couldn't see much that happened next. Fire rain? More like a fire-nami, wiping out everything. I saw Spider-Man and that rainbow-glowing gauntlet tossed through the air like a just-deflated balloon, then hurled, uncharacteristically, to the ground.

But suddenly, there was a different and somehow

brighter piece of fire that rained down on the fire-rainers. Lethally crumbling that spaceship of doom and sending it to ground. I didn't know what it was, but it provided a break in the battle.

Which was really good timing, because that's when I finally got the van going, and saw those beautiful Quantum Tunnel lights illuminate.

As I now know from Hope's account, the bigger fire was none other than Carol Danvers, aka Captain Marvel. She not only turned the tide of battle, she yanked Spider-Man and the gauntlet onto Valkyrie's horse and took charge of the final move in our plan: getting the gauntlet to me.

Or should I say, getting it past a seemingly unstoppable wave of alien monsters. Captain Marvel pierced right through the battlefield like a vibranium hole puncher. Then, with the help of some powerful friends, she zipped straight toward the back of the van, gauntlet in hand.

Except then something else flew by her, even faster: a long, glowing, and pointy weapon launched straight from Thanos. Before I could say "Duck!," it ended Luis's van. RIP, my rolling, earth-tone-striped buddy. You lived a life of heroic errandry.

And the gauntlet flew back away from us, onto the ground.

At that moment, things suddenly started going really sideways. Thanos's mob was closing in, we were out of options, and even cavalry after cavalry of new heroic team-ups weren't turning the tide.

We'd tried everything. We'd fought like hell, to hell and back. We'd worked together, we'd worked individually, and we'd kicked so much bad-guy butt our feet would never heal from the bruises. Finally, I felt the weight of that soul-sinking sigh that Cap had given me back at Avengers Compound when telling me about the Battle of Wakanda.

It seemed like it was all over as Thanos came to claim the gauntlet, as Thor, Cap, Captain Marvel, and Tony each fought heroically to take it back from him. But Thanos beat them all back, finally flinging Tony to the ground with a proclamation that seemed to sum up the vibe of the moment: "I am inevitable."

He brought together those two fateful fingers for what was sure to be the Snap to End All Snaps.

Only, all he produced was a weirdly empty, metallic "clang."

And that's when Tony held up his Iron Man–suited hand, now glowing with Infinity Stones. He had used that tussle to pickpocket them all more stealthily than anyone I met at San Quentin could have dreamed of.

Even as the unimaginable energy of the six Stones was clearly overwhelming both Tony and suit, he found the strength to "snap back" at Thanos with the words "And I . . . am . . . Iron Man."

Then Tony snapped his fingers, and just like *that*, it all changed.

Thanos went down. And all of Thanos's soldiers, dogs, and . . . whatevers . . . went down. Along with the repulsive Leviathans they rode in on. They all crumbled into that existential "cosmic dust" Thanos had reduced so many of us to so recently.

But unlike us, never to reassemble again.

That was a good moment. A great moment. On paper, the greatest I've ever experienced or ever likely will experience in my life.

We'd . . . *actually done it*. The harebrained scheme I came up with while pacing around Avengers Compound. The Scott Lang heist of a thousand lifetimes. The thing that fixed it all. It worked.

But to me, it was also one of the most terrible moments.

Because, just as Thanos and his army dissipated, for good . . .

Okay, here's where this gets hard. Almost impossible for me to type. Putting it in words makes it too real, too permanent. After all my talk of "do-overs" and second chances, some things happen only once and stay that way. And it sucks.

I know this is the last part of the big story you were counting on me to tell. What the Avengers asked me to tell. Probably, the main reason you bought the book.

But I don't want to describe it. I don't want to relive it, even in my mind. In fact, I'm going to pull rank and declare that I don't need to. The final moments of Iron Man—the original Avengers-assembler himself—are best left unspoken.

But there's really just one critical thing you, Dear Reader, need to know about what happened that day:

Tony Stark—a man who either had, or could have had, literally anything he wanted in the world—instead gave up his life to save the world.

There are no words that can capture that feeling. There's no way for me—or anyone, really—to count how many perished on that field or in the rest of the galaxy, with so many heroes trying to stop Thanos. All I know is, the sacrifices were unmistakably heroic, and clear and obvious to all.

But possibly only a dad who had lost time with a little girl so many times, who had just a tiny shot at a life with her, fully grasped what *else* Tony Stark was giving up.

And it kills me even more—I can barely write this

without tearing up—to think that, knowing all that, knowing and feeling all the same things that I feel about that, Tony *still* chose to be a self-sacrificing hero.

The guy who needed to show up and step up and do the job, right then and there.

And he did.

So in the end, our world got back half of its people . . . but lost a truly great man.

AGES OF LANG

EVER WISH YOU COULD be a different age? Little kids want to be big kids, big kids want to be teens, teens want to be young adults, and after that, everybody wants to be young again. Seems like the hair is always less gray on the other side of the fence.

A few years ago, I got a very brief, but highly memorable, chance to go on a whirlwind tour of other ages. And here's my takeaway: Nice to visit, wouldn't want to live there.

It was right before the big Infinity Stone heist I just described, when we were still working out the whole "alternate timeline" thing. Bruce, Natasha, Cap, and I were at Avengers Compound. I had come back from the Quantum Realm with some observations of how time could work differently at subatomic level. Bruce had figured out to translate them into actual, working technology. He'd reengineered the Quantum Tunnel that Hank Pym had installed in the back of Luis's van into a directed portal that, in theory, could send a person anywhere . . . er, any*when*. Tony hadn't yet come back to get it working, so we were still in the trial and error phase. And guess whose job it was to be the error?

We gave it a first shot. I was sucked into the Quantum Tunnel and spit back out. In front of me were the other three, all staring wide-eyed. At first I didn't know why, only that they seemed weirdly taller than before.

But I definitely knew something was different about me.

I said, "Uh, guys? This doesn't feel right." And then I heard how high my voice was when I said that. How it almost . . . cracked.

I was Teenage Scott!

Then they asked, "Is that Scott???" And I was so infuriated, I roared—well, more like squeaked—back, "*Yes,* it's Scott." And then suddenly, I was sucked back into the tunnel.

Well, clearly that incarnation of me wasn't going to work for the Avengers' plan. But the next me that came out was even worse.

When I popped back out of the Quantum Tunnel this time, once again I got strange looks from my comrades.

And then I felt the aches and pains. I mean, beyond the usual ones. Aches and pains I can handle. I've been in prison. I've been in Super Hero battles. I have bruises in places it's not even possible to suntan.

But this had a different texture to it. This was the pain of being worn-out and used up. All at once I realized: I must have come back as Old Man Scott.

I helpfully let my teammates know: "Oh . . . my back!"

Bruce responded by banging on his console a few times, until suddenly, again, *Zap! Suck!*

Moments later, I was popped back out once again. Now that space helmet felt gigantic around my head. And the air blowing around inside the helmet was cooling off my . . . apparently suddenly bald head? It was *so frigging weird*. And all I wanted to do was offer my own, college-trained scientific observation: "Guys, this is *so frigging weird!*"

But agonizingly, I couldn't form a word to save my life.

I stared at my friends' eyes again, and this time they had yet another look. I'll call it "freaked out in a different way, but also super-affectionate."

Right. So now apparently I was Baby Scott. And in that moment, all I could think was, "How did the Hulk turn me into a baby? Will I be a baby forever? Am I the Hulk's baby?"

My one condition for agreeing to the experiment described in this essay was that the Avengers take my photo next to the giant "A" on their wall. And you know? Worth it.

One more suck back in, one more try from Bruce's machines, and finally *Now* Me was back. With a freshly "moistened" set of pants.

Now of course that wasn't the last breakthrough we needed. It would still take a whole new level of tech from Tony, later, to actually direct us usefully through quantum space to get those Stones. But at least we'd conquered the "age-traveling" problem. I was back to the same age, same size, same everything as before.

And yet . . .

Later on (after we had safely put Thanos & co. in the rearview mirror), I was still thinking about those few moments of dramatic transformation. Experiencing life, with my fully conscious, present-day-adult-Scott brain but inside those Scott-at-different-ages-of-life bodies, had changed me. I wasn't really quite the same at all.

Take my brief foray into adolescence. Even before my higher-pitched teen voice piped up to say it, I could already tell that something didn't quite "feel right."

I know because what I felt was this sudden wave of contempt for my Super Hero friends. Now the only thing I saw them as was "super-annoying grown-ups." They just seemed to be so *alien* to me, almost intolerably so. My body was itching to get me away from them, into my own space, so I could just do my thing.

What I've realized since then is that this feeling was basically evolution at work. This is how adolescents break away from dependence on their parents and develop the drive to become self-sufficient adults. It's like nature's "repulsor technology."

And that's helped shed new light on all the times that Cassie has acted like this around me. Shutting me out, if not outright fleeing my presence. I have felt so hurt by those reactions—*after all the time we missed together, how can she not want to spend every second with me?*

Now of course I know what teenagers generally think of adults, especially the ones they're related to. But it's been a while since my teenage years, and what this experience gave me was a fresh jolt of "what it all *feels* like." It helps me realize that, as hurtful as it can be in the moment, my Cassie's chilliness toward her dad is natural and, frankly, healthy.

So thanks to this experience, I finally was able to let go of all that pain from my daughter's teenage years. Quite a journey for a few seconds in a spacesuit!

As for being Old Scott, I don't exactly remember a feeling (other than that back pain, of course). What I remember instead was what I saw in my friends' eyes.

When they first caught a look at Old Me, there was this extra touch of disturbance I saw in their expressions.

At the time, I just assumed it was mounting frustration. After all, this experiment we were undertaking was literally of universal importance, yet here we were, failing. Again. In a big way.

But later on, when I thought more about it, I wondered if there was something more to that brief flash of pain I spotted among their otherwise businesslike frowns.

I wonder if what they saw in me was an aged version of themselves. The cold, brutal fact that one day, old age would hit them, too. And then, the thing that . . . comes after that.

A Super Hero is theoretically always prepared for death while in action. But when it comes to life span (or as many see it, the amount of time they get to stick around and do good), reminders of that finitude can hurt.

Anyway, that's just speculation on my part. What I *can* say for sure is, rocketing from middle age to teenage to old age in the span of a minute was one of the weirdest and most disorienting experiences of my life. And mind you, I'm a guy who's *used* to suddenly shifting my size between "cashew" and "skyscraper." But this time, it wasn't just my relative proportion to the world that was changing. It was all the vastly different chemical, hormonal, and emotional stuff churning around inside me that made me feel like an actual different person each time.

And that's something else I've held on to from that experience: the very bewildering but I think ultimately wise insight that you can, and will, be a radically different person throughout your life—and yet you will still always be you.

Which brings us back to the beginning—at least my beginning—when I came out as Baby Scotty. That was an even more confusing barrage of sensory strangeness. Babies are just not people yet—they're like petri dishes of future, barely formed human stuff. Which—and again, I apologize for the scientific jargon—feels *so frigging weird*.

But there was at least one feeling I could pick up on that has stayed with me.

Just as in the previous two times, even with this verbal impasse, somehow my adult brain and memories were still intact. I knew and understood everything that was going on, but I couldn't make my body say or do a damn thing. I was in a cutting-edge, twenty-first-century super-suit that normally gives one super-human strength, agility, and endurance. And I was completely helpless.

I'll never forget that feeling of helplessness; it was absolutely *terrifying*.

And I realized that this is what most of the "civilian" world must feel when facing the mortal threats we Super Heroes tend to take for granted. Going forward,

I pledged to not only save people's bodies, but to do all I could to swaddle their fears with all my powers of reassurance, comfort, and strength.

So what do I take away from all those sharp, confusing gut-punches of feeling I got?

Believe it or not, a kind of a breakthrough. Even though I had experienced these Alterna-Scotts for just seconds, each had left me with an indelible impression: *I was all of them, all at once.*

Maybe this was just the quantum physics talking, but I saw that I was always a different me, depending on when I was observed.

And that—more so than any of Bruce's devices—gave me the clarity to find my way to the *right* me.

But take it from me: You don't need to experiment with quantum physics to get that insight for yourself. You already contain so many more versions of you than you can imagine. You just need to locate them, accept their benefits and liabilities, and turn those into the best mixture of yous possible. Because that's the you that the world needs now.

You've got it all inside you. You just need to learn to let it out.

Except, of course, that liquid coming out of Baby You.

FAAMQ

Some questions I get a lot are quick to answer.

Q. *Can you explain exactly how the Time Heist worked?*

A. No, I cannot.

Q: *Is all this size-shifting going to cause permanent damage to your body?*

A: Great question! Apparently Pym Particles can have an effect on brain chemistry, but Hank designed the Ant-Man helmet to prevent that, and I always wear it because my brain's already been through enough. But otherwise, according to my physician, all my "numbers" remain the same.

With the possible exception of my cholesterol, but that's due less to the Ant-Man suit than to the all-too-easy availability of pizza.

Q: *How on Earth are you supposed to find parking in San Francisco?*

A: Let's just say, there are many advantages to being able to shrink your car.

FAREWELL, NAT

AS FIRST IMPRESSIONS GO, I got a pretty clear one of Natasha Romanoff, aka "Black Widow," in our first encounter.

She and I were at Leipzig-Halle Airport, on opposite sides of that nasty intra-Avengers divide a few years ago. The battle had brought me face-to-face with her, and—knowing so very little about Black Widow's capabilities—I said something that makes me laugh to this day: "Look, I really don't want to hurt you. . . ."

Nat replied, "I wouldn't stress about it."

Then there were no more words.

She went all-in on me, landing a solid kick right in my most delicate spot. Followed by three more blows than I could follow. I went tiny and managed to flip her. Still at ant size, I tried pulling her arm behind her, when suddenly, *ZZZAP!* An electric shock from her Black Widow's Bite (a high-tech defense system surrounding her wrists) blew me clear of her and splatted me into something hard and metallic.

That was, literally and figuratively, a shock—but not to anyone else who knew and had worked with Nat. It seemed like everyone had a story about her. Or dozens.

Cap couldn't stop talking about her jaw-dropping exploits on missions. There was the time he, she, and Sam were trying to stop the Winter Soldier, but only Nat was able to fake out the soldier, then get close enough to land on his shoulders and wrap a choke cord around his neck.

Or the time the three of them were in Scotland, trying to save Wanda and Vision (and the Mind Stone in his head) from Thanos's hench-creeps. Cap, Falcon, and Wanda, of course, got in a few good shots. But once again, only Nat got right in there and managed to stab the bruiser named Corvus with his own glowing scepter—prompting a hasty bad-guy retreat.

Clint, too, had been in action with Nat a lot. Heck, they'd started their working relationship off with him being ordered to assassinate her!

But nowadays, he couldn't help rattling off her greatest hits. He regaled me with the time the two of them were trying to get ahold of the Regeneration Cradle before Ultron could get his shiny hands on it. How Nat rode a motorcycle right from the Quinjet onto a busy highway, retrieved Cap's shield from snarling traffic, evaded an explosion by sliding her cycle sideways, jumped into a truck to get the Regeneration Cradle, then finally "rode" that giant piece of high-tech machinery, midair, into the Quinjet from an exploding flying truck.

All in about ten minutes.

But I want to tell you something more about Nat: what she was like when she *wasn't* kicking butt.

Now admittedly, I never got to know Nat that well. But when the Avengers asked me to tell their story to the world, they made sure to fill me in on everything they could about the Avenger who never made it home.

It wasn't always easy to learn about her. Even to those who knew her best, Natasha Romanoff was always a woman of secrets. Secret past, secret family, surprisingly even a secret dislike of shawarma. Secrecy was part of her mystique.

And it was often one of her greatest weapons. After all, her first introduction to Tony Stark was infiltrating his company and spying on him by pretending to be his new assistant, "Natalie Rushman." Not many people can pull one over on Tony Stark. Nat was not many people.

And of course it's pretty much Avengers legend at this point how, during their days as a fledgling team, Nat managed to wrest mission-critical information out of Loki by deceiving him about her true intentions.

Let me repeat that: *Natasha Romanoff once managed to trick the universe's greatest trickster.*

In a lighter vein, Cap told me about how, when the two of them were trying to neutralize the Winter Soldier threat, they were on the run from what they'd just learned was a compromised S.H.I.E.L.D. They had to go incognito to a mall and hack into S.H.I.E.L.D. computers while pretending to be a newly engaged couple. As usual, Nat committed to the role above and beyond, even stopping on an escalator to plant what Cap later described to me as an "extremely convincing" kiss on him to evade detection.

And for every war story Cap had about fighting alongside Nat, he had another of her just being . . . well, *alongside* at critical and painful moments. He remembered Nat's quiet strength and presence at multiple times, whether watching Nick Fury appear to die on the operating table, or being a comfort during the emotional funeral of his decades-ago-but-lost-to-time true love Peggy Carter.

Clint, too, presented a different side of Nat. He spoke of how, after the Blip took away his entire family, he dealt with his grief by spiraling into bloody vigilantism. Then one night in Tokyo, he'd just finished taking out a yakuza crime boss and his minions, and saw a figure waiting for him. It was Nat, come to sell him on my Time Heist idea and the possibility of undoing the Snap.

Clint was struck by the fact that Nat could have easily joined the fight, either dispatching the thugs more

Natasha was such a woman of mystery, it was hard for me
to even find a photo of her.

quickly or stopping Clint in his tragedy-crazed tracks.

Instead, she just . . . waited him out, until he was calm enough to truly hear her.

In one of my few moments with Natasha, I too saw the power of her quiet strength and empathy. When I first showed up at Avengers Compound after escaping the Quantum Realm, I could see there had been tears in Nat's eyes. I couldn't imagine the burden she'd laid upon herself those past five years of still trying to save a half-liquidated world. But somehow she held it all in there, together.

Of all the fights he's been in with her (next to and sometimes against), Clint said the one that struck him the most was the fight Nat chose not to have.

The two of them were on the planet Vormir, carrying out their Time Heist assignment to retrieve the Soul Stone.

The being guarding the stone—Clint described him as a "big red floating guy"—explained that the only way to obtain that stone was to leave a life behind. Someone would have to sacrifice their own life for the (very much at that moment non-guaranteed!) chance to save billions.

And that's when things got *really* intense. Clint and Nat, these friends who had come to the brink of death so many times together, were now faced with a literal brink and the unavoidable death of one of them. But which one?

Clint felt powerfully that at long last, it was finally time for someone else to save Nat. And furthermore, that his life at this point was undeserving of yet one more Nat-save. He reminded her of what he'd become since the Snap, and how death was an appropriate remedy for him.

Then Nat said something that pierced more precisely into Clint than any of his arrows could have: "I don't judge people on their worst mistakes."

Clint pretended to accept her decision—and then tripped her, prepared to make his own leap, and left her with what he thought would be his last words: "Tell my family I love 'em."

And that, Clint believes, is what ultimately cast the die for Nat. Clint had a family to go love. And so did Nat: the Avengers. And this was how she was going to show her love to them.

Put Natasha Romanoff's physical prowess together with that love, and you've got the universe's most unstoppable force. She charged for the cliff. The two struggled, but Clint said that in the end, Natasha just couldn't be held back.

Even the normally granite-faced Clint started to tear up as he recalled his and Nat's last moment together, dangling from her grappling hook cord on the side of the cliff, Clint iron-gripping Nat's hand to keep her from falling.

Of course she ultimately prevailed, escaping his fingers and plummeting into both sacrifice and history. Nat's last words in this life were *Let me go.*

Which, to Clint, sounded less like, "Loosen your grip," and more like what he—and really everyone I spoke to—agreed could have been Nat's life motto:

"Allow *me* to be the one who goes."

After hearing all these stories, I wish I'd gotten to spend more time with Nat. Gotten to know her better, to the extent anyone could.

But even my few, brief encounters with Natasha Romanoff were as super-charged as her electrified wrists. So I'm really grateful to the Avengers for giving me this chance to experience through their eyes what it was like to live, work, and fight alongside a legend.

And speaking of fights and wrist shocks, if you're somehow reading this somewhere, Nat, don't worry about that first tussle we had.

Because in the end, the only person who got hurt was me, for not getting to be your pal.

GO BIG, THEN GO HOME

BEYOND HEARING THE AVENGERS' full story, I suspect there's at least one other reason you bought this book (unless you're a friend or family member that I guilted into coming to a book signing). It's because you're curious to hear what it's like to be small.

But I have a saying: *To know what it is to be small, you must first know what it is to be big.*

So I also want to share what "going ginormous" in the Ant-Man suit feels like—from inside the suit—because, like so many things I've experienced, it's given me a new perspective. Specifically, that getting big can be extremely dangerous. But not only in the way you might think . . .

GIANT LAB RAT

My first bout with enlargement was in Hank Pym's lab. This one had been built with super-high ceilings for this exact purpose. And I was a little nervous.

I hit the regulator button and BOOM! Big Me. Now I had been expecting the sudden shoot up into the air. What I didn't expect was that I would suddenly feel off-balance. I began to teeter, which is the last thing you want when you're in a position to squash tens of millions of dollars' worth of equipment plus an amazing woman you really, really want to love you.

Even worse, on the inside I was flailing for emotional balance. Every (suddenly enlarged) fiber of me was screaming, "This was a mistake!" What if my body just couldn't handle this? What if I returned to my original size permanently damaged from the experiment?

And worst of all, what if I let down Hope, and Hank? Here I was, on the cusp of being handed a new shot at life—one that basically no one else, not my ex-wife or prospective employers, was willing to give me. What if I just couldn't become this hero that two strangers, improbably, were trying to make me into? What if I was forced back into a life of crime, because maybe I really didn't have any other use in the world?

Then I remembered something: how I'd first gone small, when I fooled around with the Ant-Man suit I'd pilfered from Hank's safe and hit the shrink button. That was nothing short of *terrifying*. Within the space of a few minutes, I was nearly drowned, crushed, stabbed by a phonograph needle, and crushed again.

But what I remembered was, when that happened, little old "no-good" ex-con me had pulled some fast moves, kept my wits about me, and emerged from that in one piece—and ready to fight another day.

I now realized that day had come, and that I was indeed ready. I knew that I could be as big on the inside as I was on the outside.

And then the experimental effects hit my brain and I passed out—but with a tiny/huge smile on my face.

GIANT IN GERMANY

My next outing as Big Me came when I was thrust into that epic intra–Super Hero throwdown at Leipzig-Halle Airport. It was a brutal scene all around. Our team was taking it hard. We needed a Hail Mary. And I quickly realized it was sitting right there in that dime-sized red button on my glove.

However, truth be told, I was still doubting myself on the inside. Even though I'd mentally pulled it together at Pym Labs, I still wasn't able to physically stay on my feet for more than a few minutes. That was not a ton of battle time. I was already mentally gaming out a best-case scenario of how many combatants I could take down before I fainted this time. I wasn't feeling optimistic.

And then Cap said three words that changed everything: "Are you sure?"

Not exactly an inspiring speech from a football coach in a movie, but, as I hope I've made clear by now, when one of the bravest men on the planet gives you a "Yes or No" choice, for me, that's not a choice.

I hit the button.

But unlike in the lab trial, now there was no time—or mental bandwidth, really—to focus on my feelings.

Because now, *everything* was suddenly happening to me—all at once! One second I was midair, clutching War Machine's ankle, the next I was swinging him through the air by his. I was attempting to clobber the King of Wakanda by kicking a bus. I had Spider-Man in my eye. Then I had Vision passing *through* my innards!

And then I felt my legs start to lock up, and as before in the lab, I began to stagger. But it wasn't for the same reason this time. My head was still (relatively) clear. No, this was a loss of balance being deliberately brought on by Spider-Man tying a web rope around my legs and blabbing on about *The Empire Strikes Back*. (Which, by the way, excellent taste, kid.)

Then, out of nowhere, Rhodey and Tony Stark gave me a double-KO punch, and I was going down. For the record, it is *way* more unsettling to be helplessly plummeting to the ground when you're fully awake for it.

And that was nothing compared to what my body felt when it made full contact with the tarmac. I can't even count how many kinds of pain my giant-sized nervous system was taking in.

But you know where I *was* feeling good? In my heart.

Sure, I'd once again only lasted a few minutes at Jumbo Scale before taking a fall. But this time, I'd fallen in *battle*. A battle where I (again, until recently a guy no one would even trust to scoop ice cream) had pounded some formidable foes—and even better, come through for my friends.

I quickly reverted to standard size, but in my mind, I was still feeling like a giant.

SAN FRANCISCO GIANT (GO TEAM!)

If I learned one thing from my first two enlargements, it was "choose a softer surface to crash onto." Enter: San Francisco Bay.

This time, the feeling was completely different. I had a little more suit-experience under my belt. Also, I didn't have a cavalcade of butt-kicking heroes assaulting me. And finally, my mission in this case was a lot more specific, quicker, and literally smaller! All I had to do was grab a tiny lab shrunken down to the size of a suitcase.

So I was feeling confident. But perhaps . . . a bit more confident than I should have. (We can blame Cap for that!) I went big, inside and out, assured I could handle anything. And I did manage to get my massive hands on the tiny lab. Success!

However, I only know this because—as endless loops of local news footage reminded me later—I loudly bragged about it like a drunken sailor to a deck full of terrified ferry passengers. I'd let my temporary god-mode go to my head. And my head was actually the main issue right then! Because my brain wasn't getting enough oxygen, a problem I knew about with Giant Man–mode but had failed to take seriously or train myself for. Apparently,

I had overcompensated for my past doubts by shifting all the way over into thinking I was invincible.

And that's when the air in my suit told me otherwise. As I gasped desperately to breathe, I found myself once again being forcibly brought back down to earth (well, technically, down into the Bay).

A softer landing, yes—but personally, a harder fall.

I don't remember this moment very well, so I'm very grateful to whichever local news copter took this photo.

GIANT VS. THANOS

But fear not. I was saved from what could have been a permanent fish-nap by Hope. Apparently it takes more than three falls to keep a good, constantly size-shifting man down.

Which is a good thing, because not long after that, I emerged from the Quantum Realm and found myself in a Blipped world in need of a big solution.

I've already detailed the circumstances that brought me there, and what went down after. But for now, I just want to note that the big battle with Thanos was the very first time in my brief but extremely eventful heroing career when I'd finally found out how to be big the right way.

Obviously, there were external differences. I was in better shape, and the adrenaline of facing down basically Armageddon in upstate New York overrode my emotions. (It also didn't hurt that, unlike in Germany, I was actually fighting on the same side as all my colleagues.)

So there I was, slipping back and forth between big and small mode, rescuing my pals from the rubble of Avengers Compound, and then racing into the battle of my life on my titanic feet. I crushed one of Thanos's soldiers, and didn't bat an eye when I came face-to-face with one of his massive Leviathans.

This time I didn't give myself mental space for either doubt or braggadocio. I just went for it.

And when my left uppercut connected with that giant Robo-Kaiju-Lizard, he went down so fast, that rush gave me the energy to stay on my feet longer than I had ever managed before this point.

But the real difference—the thing that I'd retained despite multiple blows to the head and one near-drowning—was that this time, I finally knew when to *stop* being big.

GIANT FINAL THOUGHTS

And that's the lesson I took away from all this. Getting to step into significantly larger shoes—whether literally or just in our ordinary lives—can have two equally dangerous effects on our psyches. We can shrink in self-doubt from what we're truly capable of. Or we can inhabit our new power boldly, but forget the humble size we began as.

Because, at some point in our lives, or maybe two, or three, most of us get the chance to be "the big one" relative to someone else. We just find ourselves there, whether it's on the playground or the break room or just being around our kids. For a lot of people, it can be overwhelming, as it was for me.

But the scarier part is, for many it can also be straight-up *addictive*.

Even the most diminutive of us, at some moment, has someone else's life, or status, or feelings in our hands. And even if that wasn't our doing, but just how the cards were dealt, we should never view that situation as anything but temporary. After all, the next day, we might be the ones under someone else's thumb. (For a guy who frequently goes small like me, that's not just a metaphor!)

Which is exactly why we should never get too attached to our dominance, or make that our outlook on others and the world. We should never exploit that extra piece of "bigness" for small reasons.

And we should definitely never ever use that bit of leverage to try and make ourselves even bigger. Because that's just not how we humans were meant to be, or how we work best. I have a lab floor, airport tarmac, and a part of the San Francisco Bay that will attest to this.

That is why I'm actually glad that the Ant-Man suit doesn't make it possible for me to stay large too long. Admittedly, this can make combat trickier (or, to be more precise, *shorter*), but it also keeps my perspective wiser: It literally doesn't let me get a big head.

So, in a way, this brings me full circle:

To know how to be big, first you must remember what it's like to be small.

FAAMQ

Q: *We have a major ant infestation but don't want to have an exterminator fill our house with poison. Could you come . . . talk to them?*

A: Boy, would I love to. There are few greater rushes I get than from sending out those olfactory signals and watching the little guys get into lockstep formation and listen to my every word. They are possibly the only sentient creatures in my life who do.

Unfortunately, I've learned the hard way that I can't ask them to do *too* much. They are, after all, independent beings with their own biological imperatives and agendas—you know, just living their best ant lives! And my typical requests take them away from that. So I have to be extremely selective with what I ask of them. Otherwise, the next time I need a high-security duct infiltrated or a signal decoy stolen, they might just spell out the words "Do It Yourself, Two-Legs."

So I'd say, look at where they're coming in and seal that off, and eliminate any spilled food or water that might be drawing them in. And yeah, you also might want to try some lemon juice.

REGRETS?
I'VE HAD A TON

I HOPE BY NOW we've gotten comfortable enough for me to lay something on you that's so shocking, I'm struggling to even type out the words. . . .

I've made a few mistakes in my time.

Okay, maybe more than a few.

But fortunately, I've learned a few things from those mistakes along the way. And even more fortunately for you, I love to share!

NO MORE POOL PARTIES!

For instance, take my whole "incident" with my former employer, the secretly-embezzling-millions VistaCorp. Do I regret getting caught? Every single day. Do I regret the hack itself? Never. That was the part I got right. Because, just like the actions I take part in when my fellow heroes' fists, feet, and capes are flying, there are key moral values at play: *Protect the innocent. End the aggression. Restore justice.*

But . . . at the same time, I've also come to understand my real mistake.

It wasn't breaking into VistaCorp's servers to return the money they stole from customers. That's where I should have quit while I was ahead.

No, my mistake was making the whole operation into the "Scott Lang Good Times Hero Hour." I had already blown the whistle. I could have just stolen the money from VistaCorp and quietly returned it to the victims. But instead, I had to show off, post all the bank records online, and drive a car into a pool. I turned what could have been a private, quiet moment of doing the right thing into three years away from my kid.

LOVE MEANS ALWAYS HAVING TO SAY YOU'RE SORRY

A lot of people have asked me how I managed to ruin a perfectly good marriage with Maggie. Well, I've given this a lot of thought over a lot of time, and I've finally come to understand what my biggest actual mistake was in this case.

It was not sharing with my life partner *everything*. Not just my own "plans" regarding VistaCorp. That was more like the final straw in a lot of "strategic miscommunications" on my part. I don't want to get into our personal details, but I've had to take a good hard look at what I chose to share versus what I believed myself entitled to decide on my own—even if those decisions impacted our family.

But then of course I wouldn't be with Hope. But . . . but . . . but . . . you see how easy it is to fall into the regrets trap? It's a bottomless pit. And the only way to find the bottom is to decide for ourselves when we've done enough beating ourselves up.

FIGHTING THE GOOD FIGHT . . . BADLY

Another bad move buried inside a good move was how I handled the big airport fight in Germany. Of course, I don't mean the "going to fight at an airport in Germany" step. I'm still good with that decision. I stood up for Cap in his hour of need, and I also managed to get in some valuable "networking" with future Avengers colleagues!

Nor—and this is still painful—do I completely regret doing this in secret from Hank and Hope, with equipment I stole from them. In fairness, there was just no way I could have told them. If they were caught and questioned about it—and admitted they knew what I was up to and didn't stop me—they'd be liable as accomplices. Which would extra piss off Hope because she prefers to think of *me* as the accomplice.

However, as far as the stealing itself . . . I have to admit it, I do still feel pretty damn awful about that. All I can say in my defense is two things: One, wearing the Ant-Man suit was clearly what my new Super Hero pals wanted from me. Two, at the very least, after the mission (and after a fun little stay in that very secret, very wet Super Hero prison under the East River) I did sneak the suit back to Luis in a trophy, (relatively) unstained and in one piece. Which is more than I can say for the tailbone I landed smack on!

And funnily enough, that epic fall was also exactly where my mistake landed. Because you see, the reason

I got knocked down so easily was—just as with my little amphibious-car-driving adventure—I decided to show off instead of just show up.

There I was, at Leipzig-Halle Airport, fighting in that—for lack of a better term—"civil war." A lot was going on, *really* fast, but basically, it wasn't going well for my side. Cap and Bucky desperately needed to get out of there and to Siberia before it was too late, but they were pinned down.

Sam said on his wrist-com, "We need a diversion. Something big." Well, I immediately took that as my cue. *Yes, Scott! You can do "big." Now's your chance to impress these guys and prove you belong in their ranks.*

You see how fast my brain was racing here? Before I knew it, I was giving battlefield commands as if I was Captain America, and promising the use of a still-quite-experimental technique that I really did not have a handle on.

So, in the end, was it a mistake for me to go giant right then? Not entirely. Ultimately, I *did* manage to divert many of our (then) opponents. Cap and Bucky *did* get away as planned. And I *did* manage to not pass out (only to be knocked onto my butt in a completely different way).

The thing is, it was also an *extremely* risky call on my

part. Brave and creative, sure. Wise? Not so clear, in hindsight. I really didn't know what I was doing with the enlargement feature, and I didn't have Hank or Hope around to offer guidance. A thousand things could have gone wrong, not only for me, but for the allies I was trying to help. I think the best thing you could say is, it was a decision made for not all the best reasons . . . that ended up with me getting lucky.

And in a line of work where people often live or die based on the quality of decision-making, that's not good enough. At least for me.

But that's where I want to draw a key distinction. I look back at that airport decision not with regret, but with hard introspection. The difference is, regret traps us. Introspection frees us.

GAME ON!

So as a thought exercise, I decided to reflect on how a few key moments in my life would have turned out if I'd made different choices.

And to help me with that, I checked in with the world's most highly skilled "gaming it out" expert, my former cell mate, current colleague, and perpetual pal, Luis.

When I first asked him this, he just gave me that "Luis look." As if to say, *Hasn't your life been crazy and complicated*

enough, without introducing alternate directions and endings?
He packs a lot into those looks. And in a way, he's already
gotten the point of this essay. But let's hear how Luis
broke down how I handled VistaCorp.

Luis said, "All right. Let's say you *didn't* make such a
public show of what you were doing—driving that sweet
car into a pool, sharing the bank records with the whole
damn internet, and such."

I was smiling, remembering the feeling. Then Luis's
snapping fingers snapped me back into focus.

He continued, "In that case, maybe the boss man might
have had a chance to catch wind of this before it went
big. That would also have given him a chance to put his
fall guys in place, and potentially slip through the fingers
of the law. So in that scenario, maybe his ride stays dry,
and you walk free!"

I had to admit, that sounded pretty good. Or at least
preferable to three years in San Quentin.

But Luis wasn't done. "Which would also *also mean*
Hank Pym would never learn of your existence, so he
ends up hiring some less talented con, they mess up the
Pym Tech heist, and now Darren Cross is running his
own private army."

Yikes.

But Luis *still* wasn't done!

"But above and beyond all that," he wrapped up, "is the greatest tragedy of all time: You don't go to prison—and *you and I don't get to be besties!*"

After the kind of hug that that response required, I reminded Luis that "Also . . . the whole universe would have been destroyed?"

Then he brought me in for another hug, looked me in the eye, and murmured, "That's what I just said, amigo."

Okay, no one warned me how emotionally taxing introspection can be! But I was in for the whole experience now. I decided to test out how I could have handled the whole "Maggie communication" issue.

Luis set the scene. "Imagine a younger Scott, sitting across the kitchen table from your still-then-wife Maggie. You've got something big to share. You take both of Maggie's hands in yours and you just . . . tell her. Like, everything. All the really bad stuff VistaCorp is up to. And then—here's the bigger deal—what you plan to do about it."

Yeah. That was definitely the "bigger deal." If Maggie had had any notion of what lengths I was willing to go to . . .

Luis kept spinning out the angle. "So then Maggie's still sitting there, taking this all in, her hands still in yours. And then suddenly, she flips your hands around so yours are captive in hers."

Wait, *what now?*

"Then in the blink of an eye, she uses her elbow to turn on the electric stove, and before you can figure out what's going on, Maggie has scalded your fingertips!"

I was pretty close to lost at this point, but Luis brought it home.

"So now for at least a month, you can't type a single keystroke. As a hacker, you're useless!"

I didn't even know what to do with that. The message that Luis's earlier look had conveyed—that this way lay madness—was starting to become very clear.

Luis saw my look of bewilderment (and phantom finger-pain) and smiled. "But hey, on the bright side, no divorce, and you never lose Cassie!"

Then our smiles paled as this time we both realized the irreducible emotional complexity of this imagined timeline.

Yes Cassie. But . . . no Luis. Yes universe. And no universe.

I grabbed Luis another beer and gave him permission to stop thinking now.

You see, this is where things always end up when I try

to imagine alternate futures or pasts while consumed with regret. Too much changes, too many things can go wrong, and pretty soon even the people you thought you knew and cared for become unrecognizable. It's impossible to know what the exact best call is in the moment. But as I said, that's a big part of the job of being a Super Hero. That's why I've tried to break through the wall of regretting decisions into the more powerful place of improving *how* I make decisions.

And I don't regret that one bit.

FAAMQ

Q: *Can you introduce me to the Avengers?*

A: Man, if I had a nickel for every time I got asked this . . . I could pretty much buy my own Quinjet.

So, in brief, sorry, not really. As you might imagine, being Super Heroic also means they're all super-busy. Clint also has his hands full with his family and a new protégé. And Bruce? I never know where (like, even on what world) he is, but he's always busy.

You didn't hear this from me, but if you really want to meet a Super Hero, may I humbly suggest putting yourself in mortal danger from an otherworldly being?

LOOK-OUT-FOR-THE-LITTLE GUIDE

EVEN WHEN I'M NOT in giant form, I tend to have a big mouth.

I know I've been talking a big game about acting metaphorically big or little. And obviously, there's the title I chose for this book. (Well, technically, my publisher chose it. I wanted to call it *Ant Misbehavin'*.)

But for real, to me this stuff is more than just a series of empty platitudes. I honestly feel like we're stuck in a world of people trampling on those they consider beneath them. And as a guy who spends a lot of time down at ant-level, I am very much "anti-trample."

So now I'm going to tell you *how* to look out for the little guy. But in what you've come to recognize as a signature Scott Lang move, first . . . I'm going to talk about me.

Because long before I opened Hank Pym's basement vault, I felt like an extremely tiny guy myself.

And I'm not talking about how I didn't even get my growth spurt until *age fourteen*. That's right. My best position on the basketball court was "statistician."

No, I mean in my adult life—like at VistaCorp. When I caught wind of how this company I worked for was ripping off their customers, I was outraged. I'd seen how much my boss was raking in, and I felt rage on behalf of all those folks who'd put their trust and, of course, money into my place of business.

I didn't know it yet, but inside my head I was already heading down the path of recognizing who's the "little guy" in life, and feeling no choice but to stand up and fight for them. Or at least, throw off the big guy trying to hurt them.

That was what I tried to do with VistaCorp. I couldn't completely stop what they were doing, but I did manage to undo some of it . . . and then I was fired.

To the Powers That Be, I might as well have been an ant.

And boy, did I feel crushed under their patent-leather shoes when I ended up doing hard time. But what I remember from all of that is not the bitterness.

What I remember is those who looked out for me.

Calling or texting, just asking how they could help.

And then there was my first day in prison.

Take it from me: That's not an easy day for anyone of any size. But when Luis reached out to me, I felt a tiny bit better knowing I had an ally. With his support during those long, long years, months, weeks, and, let's be honest, even just many endless hours, I felt like I could make it to the other side.

Now I've worked alongside some of the strongest and bravest Super Heroes who've ever walked the earth. But the heroes that have had the largest impact on my life have been the ones with no powers other than the eyes to see a person in need, and the voice to offer words of support.

Which brings me to you. I want to tell you something important: You, in the exact life you're in right now, can be a hero, too.

You don't have to fly, punch someone three times your size, or stop a galactic Super Villain from destroying the planet to be a hero.

Because you may not have super abilities, but you

definitely already have two incredible powers: a heart to care, and a voice to speak out. All you have to do is learn to use them.

First, heart. As you make your way through your day, take note of the people who the world "shrinks." The person who foams your ridiculously complex coffee order. Who delivers the food you were too lazy to cook. Who cleans the bathroom you and a million people rush in and out of, in a hurry to catch your train.

And when I say "take note," I don't mean, like, pull out a megaphone and yell, "Here toils a person of HONOR!" Instead, I mean just . . . show them some love. A little friendly human interaction—even something as simple as a smile or a compliment on their funny T-shirt—is a way of saying, "I see you, and I don't take you for granted."

But looking out goes way beyond just being nice to people in the service industry. As I've mentioned before, we can all be made to feel small in so many different ways in life. Crushed by a piece of bad news. Made to feel less-than by another's prejudices or dismissive tone. Overworked, overstretched, overlooked. Even the people we assume have it all together, the ones we depend on, our rocks—well, sometimes, on the inside, they're barely pebbles.

It's easy to pay attention to the folks who loom large—the alpha silverback gorillas loudly beating their chests and taking up the room. The challenge is to turn your attention away from them, to the ones they're taking it away from.

The good news is, you don't need Pym Particles to instantly make someone feel bigger. Just like you can use your heart to join forces with the little guys, you can use your voice to join them on the battlefield.

To be clear, I'm not necessarily suggesting you jump in and meddle in someone's life! People's boundaries are critical and fragile, and they need to be respected. And people who are feeling small do not need a sudden, unhired publicist announcing that to the world.

Instead . . . and here I'm really pushing this metaphor

Cassie took this photo of me, and sends it as a reply text when she feels I'm acting "small." But joke's on her, because I think I look very cute here.

to its breaking point . . . hang on, metaphor, you can do this! . . . Start small.

Because folks try all kinds of ways to hide their troubles. In our world, sadly, there's nothing more "uncool" than being an actual, real-live person with real-live vulnerabilities. But ultimately, it's all visible in their eyes. And that's how you can reach someone safely, across that Curtain of Cool. Whatever their fast-moving mouth or lying smile try to tell you, you can see when something makes their gaze falter.

For instance, I can still remember this guy Lenny, who worked janitorial duty at San Quentin. That's a pretty terrible job, and I couldn't do anything to change Lenny's situation. But what I could do was greet him, every single day for three years, with a fist-bump and a sincere "Thanks, Lenny. The place looks BEAUTIFUL!" That joke never got old (or funny), but it reminded Lenny that he had humanity outside of this cage, and that someone else knew it.

We humans have gotten used to ignoring, overlooking, or flat-out denying the signal that says, "I'm in a bad place," but it's often in our faces. And there is no hiding it.

So when you detect that signal, that's your time to

move. Flash the other person a look that says, like Luis did to me, "You got this." Give them the optical assurance that they, too, will eventually emerge from the prison of their current plight.

If it's someone you regularly speak to or have interactions with, and you know in more detail what they're going through, you can also use your voice. But be tactical here as well. Don't just go for the "Is everything okay?" because that's the megaphone problem again. It might just trigger them to redouble their emotional armor and retreat further into their lonely smallness.

Instead, try something more like, "I'm here if you need me." Nine times out of ten, they won't actually take you up on the offer. Honestly, what they're most likely to pick up on are just those two powerful first words: "I'm here." Just that reminder, that they're not alone, can make someone feel like they're giant enough to tackle the challenges ahead.

Also, occasionally you might be a direct eyewitness to someone using their bigger size (or status or wealth or whatever) to make someone else feel inferior. But guess what? That voice of yours can do just as much to make someone feel big as my little blue enlarger discs.

When you see someone cutting someone else down,

whether through status, money, race, gender, or anything, even the quietest "That's not cool" or "Take it easy" can ring out louder than the Hulk stepping barefoot on a thumbtack.

It may not stop the big shot currently in mid–power trip. But it sends them a strong message. That message: "This person you're picking on has an ally now. That means they're effectively twice as big as you." Nine times out of ten, this is all it takes for a bully to back off.

But equally importantly, it sends a message to the target of their attempted cut-downs. That message: "You're not alone. In this or anything." And that—last time for this metaphor, I swear—feels *huge*.

FAAMQ

Q: *Do you do birthday parties?*

A: I would love to! However—and this is kind of embarrassing for me to admit—I've become a little traumatized by them. It all goes back to Cassie's birthday the year I got out of prison. I went over to her house to surprise her. I hadn't seen my little Peanut in three years, back when she was an even tinier legume. Can you imagine how exciting this was for me?

Sadly, it was a lot less exciting for her mom Maggie and her new almost-stepdad, who were *not* expecting me, as this didn't fall under our custody arrangement. They basically kicked me out, in full sight of a very saddened Cassie (and Daddy).

Surprise!

And then, after missing out on so many of Cassie's birthdays (between prison and being stuck in the Quantum Realm during the Blip), I made yet one more miscalculation and tried to surprise Cassie with an over-the-top birthday-stravaganza to make up for the missed ones. I'm talking mimes, eight entire cakes, and four bouncy castles—which, it turns out, was precisely four bouncy castles too many.

Because remember: At this point, Cassie was a teenage girl. So I'll leave it to your imagination how well an unexpected, huge, needy, attention-grabbing stunt from her *dad* went over. Super Hero, super cringe.

So, please, have a happy birthday! But maybe tell your friends and family, "No surprises."

ANT ON THE WALL

IT'S IRONIC.

As a kid and a teenager, I was so socially awkward, I would have killed for the power to shrink myself down to the point of invisibility. And yet, now that I'm an adult, I'm actually pretty decent at fitting in to almost any social situation.

How did I become *this* charismatic, you might ask? This power doesn't have an exciting origin story. I wasn't injected with an experimental "cool guy" serum. (Just ask my daughter!)

Instead, before I became able to "fit in" between molecules, I learned how to fit in to groups of people who were already doing their thing way before I showed up.

And that's good, because over the last ten years or so, I've had to do a *lot* of in-fitting: to a gang of, let's say, "fist-forward" fellow inmates; to a semi-awkward "post-divorce blended-family situation" with Maggie and Paxton; and of course, to the Avengers & co. That last one probably wasn't helped by the fact that I first met some of them by trying to fight them. Very hard to overlook a first impression when it's been made in your face.

So how did I learn to be the Human Puzzle Piece That Always Fits? The good news is that, while it's always a challenge, it's also totally doable—for anyone. And so I thought I'd share some pro tips. If this were a book (well, I mean, besides the one it already is), it wouldn't be so much *How to Win Friends and Influence People* as *How to Not Have People Reject You and Maybe, Maybe One Day Consider You a Friend or at Least Not a Total Creeper.*

Okay, that title could stand to have a red "shrink disc" hurled at it.

Shall we get on with the tips?

1. DON'T SPEAK

I mean, at least at first don't speak. And what I really mean is, don't enter a new group shooting your yapper off. I made that mistake in college. I knew my science-focused campus was full of smart people. But in my impetuous, cocky freshman year, I also secretly believed I was one of the *really* smart ones. And some insecure part of me worried that, if I didn't lay down that "Big Brain on Campus" marker ASAP, someone else would take the title.

But unsurprisingly, my peacock-like displays of "Fun Facts" led to social isolation (even by my uber-nerdy school's standards). So eventually I started to evolve. When I entered a new situation, I would say my name, then "Nice to meet you," and . . . that's it. At first. It was a revolutionary new technique (to me) called "Listening to what they had to say first before shooting my mouth off."

I know, I know, "be a good listener." It sounds obvious when I put it down on paper. It's just that, when you do actually know a lot of stuff—or let's say, have a lot of stuff that's just dying to be shared—it can be extremely tempting to just let the old firehose spurt!

But here's the real secret: Every group develops a sub-culture all its own, becomes its own mini-society. And if you're a late arrival, you enter speaking a different language. You need to give yourself the time to learn the new group's tongue, their pace, their sense of humor, and what they value most—and least.

So hang back, give your jaws a rest, and soon enough, your brain will automatically migrate to your new team's wavelength.

And that's an *actual* Fun Fact!

2. STOP TRYING

While we're still talking brain stuff, it turns out we humans (along with many other species) have this built-in tendency called "mirroring" that puts others at ease. When someone smiles, you smile back. When someone relaxes into their chair, you follow suit. When someone vomits, well . . . maybe it's time to leave that tailgate party.

But we also have a tendency to take it too far. Sometimes we try to *completely* replicate what others do, in order to prove that we're cut from the same cloth, on the same team. Or to use the technical term, we "suck up."

Boy, did I learn that the hard way when I first started working with the Avengers! Turns out Clint doesn't want to be repeatedly invited to "go out shootin'." Thor is *never* going to be impressed with how much Norwegian you learn online. No matter how many times you pick the right card, Wanda Maximoff is never going to believe you "know magic."

And let's be clear: You don't have to go to the other extreme either. By all means, show an interest and ask tons of questions about your new coworker's obsession with painting tiny figurines. That's the "Listen" follow-up to the "Shut Up" point above. But you don't have to show up, unannounced, at his house on a Saturday morning with a horsehair brush and a tiny overpriced dragon figure ready for a metallic finish.

3. BE "THE GUY" (OR GAL)

How high would you raise your eyebrows if I told you that, at its heart, prison is a place of kindness?

What I mean is, it's such a harsh, unforgiving, humanity-stripped-down-to-its-essentials institution, that a few kind deeds are worth a lot there.

The cliché from movies and TV shows is that surviving prison is all about asserting your dominance. Even though you may be an electrical engineer, you're supposed to somehow mosey up to the biggest bruiser there, and somehow—clean the yard with his face.

Well, I knew that was never going to fly—that the much more likely yard-cleaning would be with mine. So I tried a slightly different approach.

I would find the toughest guys and ask them when their birthdays were. Ridiculous, right? It certainly wasn't what they were expecting. But as I explained, I knew how hard it was to keep track of time in prison, so if they told me their birthdates, I'd make sure to sing "Happy Birthday" to them.

What on Earth was I thinking? Simply that everyone—even the most menacing-looking seven-foot-tall stack of muscles—wants to be treated as a full human being. And if you can find a path into that humanity, you can connect with anyone.

Beyond the birthday stuff (and man, by the end I was singing that song more often than an overworked "family-style" restaurant waiter), I was The Guy. The Guy who helped you pick up the pile of metal plates you accidentally knocked off the workbench in the shop. The Guy who noticed you in the corner, trying to keep down tears because you missed your little girl. Actually, sometimes I was also that corner guy.

The point is, when everyone around you is fighting and stealing, I was The Guy who was going the opposite route. That more than anything got me through all three years among the granddaddy of tough crowds.

And I've got the still-unbroken septum and annual birthday cards from those bruisers to prove it.

4. BUT DON'T BE "THAT GUY" (OR GAL)

The downside of this is, it can be a very slippery slope going from being the person who does something for everyone . . . to the one who *needs* something from everyone.

And right after I got released, I was pretty much a Human Pool of Need. On top of the creature comforts and freedom I'd been denied for years, I was just starving for human companionship. So I kept bugging Maggie about seeing Cassie, even when she told me repeatedly, "Not yet." Finally I couldn't stand it any longer and just showed up as an unwanted "surprise" at Cassie's birthday party.

Paxton may have been the police officer there, but it was Maggie who read me the riot act. She told me my daughter needed a dad who was stable, supportive, and on the right path in life. Not . . . whatever it was I was then. And that I could not see Cassie until I'd made some solid progress in that department.

Wow, that got me. I guess I'd always seen myself as all those good things, deep inside my own understanding of life. But from the outside, I started to see how Cassie might perceive me. Especially if I started gravitating toward Luis & co.'s criminal plans and ended up in jail again.

So that hurt. Badly. There are few things in life more devastating than suddenly noticing the huge gap between how you see yourself versus how others do.

But it was a solid wake-up call from Maggie, and made me appreciate how hard she was working to protect our daughter. A plan I can 100 percent get behind.

So I adjusted my thinking. I learned to stop seeing Maggie and Cassie and others as "Scott Fulfillers" and reminded myself that they had their own lives and needs. And it was on me to prove myself worthy of fitting in with where they were, not the other way around.

The good news is, once I found my new path (or at least, Hank put me on it), I actually ended up spending a lot more time with Cassie, Maggie, and even Paxton than I'd ever thought possible.

Which brings me to my last tip . . .

5. TIME IS ON YOUR SIDE

I mean, not biologically, of course.

But when it comes to becoming one of the gang,

sometimes you need to hit the pause button and let time work its magic.

After our little "tarmac tea party in Germany," I was ant-persona non grata for many of the Avengers & friends. Specifically, the ones I'd fought. It felt like, if I was lucky, one day they might choose to not crush me in one of their incredibly powerful hands.

But then, after my imprisonment, plea deal, and re-imprisonment in my home, I suddenly had way too much time on my hands. And time became my ally for creating allies.

As you now know, I spent a lot of that time sending out emails and texts. Sometimes just simple messages like "How's it going?" And then, in my by-now signature move, "Happy Birthday!"

That's the real irony here in all this. We've all been taught since birth that you only get things in life by working hard. However, friendship is one area where too much struggle can actually put you back further from your goal. But being patient and letting time do the work for you? That's a super-power anyone can use.

FAAMQ

Here's a few more quick hits:

Q: *Will you marry me?*

A: What a sweet note! I'm so flattered, but I'm also still definitely with Hope.

However, I will print this out for the next time we have a fight and she makes me sleep on the Ant-Couch.

Q: *When are you going to grow up, stop running around in a costume with your little friends playing "Cops and Robbers" and looking for Martians, and go back to a real job? What was wrong with the nice computer place? You were always good with computers.*

A: Hi, Mom!

FROM ANT TO MAN

ANTS ARE AWESOME.

Probably not the most unexpected sentence to hear from a guy named "Ant-Man." But it's true. They are, six legs down, the best coworkers I've ever had. And unlike other teammates I've had, with ants there's never any drama.

Now I admit, I don't have the kind of head-over-heels "affection" for ants that Hank Pym does. Part of me truly believes that—if given the zoning permit to do so—he would bulldoze his house and replace it with a giant hill.

But still, I have an awful lot of respect and admiration for the little fellas. (Or depending on my specific mission-size, just plain "fellas.") And I wanted to sing a few of their praises, because in many ways, the *Formicidae* have helped me become a better *Homo sapiens*.

First of all, ants are the ultimate *team players*. They're not the only creatures with a strong social nature, but they're up there. You've heard of "ant colonies"? Well, one species has reportedly formed a colony that's got more than 300 million ants, ranged up and down the coast of Europe. Which, to be honest, makes it sound pretty luxurious to be an ant! And just imagine how hard it must be to reach common agreement among 300 million of your fellow . . . anythings. The Avengers & co. would sometimes practically break out into a second civil war over whether to order lunch from the usual Italian place or the usual Thai place.

Now what I find most impressive is what that team-centric attitude translates into: the willingness that ants have to take on any number of crazy and grinding jobs. Every colony has a queen, mating ants, and worker ants. The worker ants are stuck with all the drudgery: feeding the larvae, taking out the trash, foraging for food, defending the colony, and even policing conflict within it. Pretty sure if there were "ant-pants" to wash, they'd have to do that, too. Little surprise that the workers doing those thankless yet essential tasks are—just as all too often with our species—the females.

But it gets even more peculiar and more thankless. Some species have what's called a "soldier ant," which is not at all the little Cap ant it sounds like. Rather, when their hill or habitat is under attack, the soldier ant's job is to block off the entry hole *with their heads.*

They pack a lot of wisdom into those teeny little bodies.

Finally, a job where my natural hardheadedness would be an asset! There's also a class called "scout ants," which neither escort old lady ants across the stream nor sell extremely tiny mint-flavored chocolate cookies. Their job is to find sources of food and leave scent trails for everyone else to follow.

And the specific ants I've had the honor of working with have had to go *way* beyond what even their complex brains could have imagined. For example, the Fire Ants built elaborate and fully functioning bridges, ladders, and rafts. The ones we call "Crazy Ants" were our electrical engineers—by which I mean, they could conduct electricity with their bodies and fry out enemy electronics! The Carpenter Ants provided my winged transport to wherever I needed. My dearly departed carpenter pal Ant-thony helped me infiltrate not one but *two* high-security installations, and even out-flew *Falcon* in battle!

Do I even need to elaborate on the ant who agreed to get large, slip on my house arrest ankle monitor, and pretend to be me—to throw off the Feds during my house arrest? That is one dude who likes to live on the edge.

The point is, no matter what size I'm currently operating at, ants inspire me to say yes to any task that comes my way. I've mentioned this tendency of mine before, but ants are one of the main reasons behind it. Whenever I have a flash of doubt or fear, I tell myself, "If a creature who's in danger of being annihilated by a flip-flop can risk it all, so can you."

More broadly, they remind me that *I'm not just doing it for me*. Somehow it's both humbling and empowering to realize that every action I take can have a mission-critical, even life-or-death impact on the series of tasks that countless of my fellow heroes are undertaking at the same time. I don't have to tell you what level of ant-guts it took for my little colleagues to jam up the gun of sociopath Darren Cross or risk self-electrocution by frying Pym Technologies' security servers. But I know that all our efforts to stop the Yellowjacket suit from decimating the world would have been sunk without each of these literally tiny tasks!

Also, when I remember that there's a whole colony of others depending on me to do my job, it just makes that job easier. You might even say, more instinctual.

Another way-cool thing ants do better than just about anyone is *communication*. Now I'm not talking about Hank's ant communication device, which uses electromagnetic waves to stimulate the ant's olfactory nerves.

But that brings up something critical I wanted to highlight: Ants don't have ears. Some species don't even have eyes. Instead, they navigate their environment, including how they interact with others, through highly advanced senses of feel and smell. They are extremely sensitive at "reading" vibrations on the ground through a special organ located under their knees. (Can you imagine? "Wow, Doris, get a load of this—you will not *believe* your kneecaps!")

And as for smell, they mostly communicate by, essentially, hurling little specialized hormonal packets through the air at each other. Not unlike how I attempted to communicate with girls back in high school by using way too much cologne. Unsuccessfully.

You know what's even cooler about those two senses, though? They're not just wild ways of reading the world beyond our familiar old workhorses, the eyes and ears. They're *completely different ways of being in the world*, and being with others. Ways that I've tried to apply to my own life.

The first one, tactility, requires an extraordinary level of sensitivity. Ground vibrations are not exactly a glaringly obvious signal (even for a Californian like me, whose toes can tell you the Richter of an aftershock). To be able to "read" a wide variety of them, you have to be really attuned to your environment—more outside of your own head, as it were.

And smell is also intriguing in a different way. In humans and ants alike, it has a strong connection to memory. Now I can't speak to how extensive ant-memories are. But I know that being really adept at olfactory communication means that you're not just thinking in the moment. You're also—in a way—thinking about the past. Unconsciously or not, it's a richer way to take in the world.

So I think being among the ants so much has heightened my facilities for sensitivity and memory. I know this because I've faced some serious communication challenges, and learning to become more sensitive to both present and past have helped me through.

Figuring things out with my ex-wife, Maggie, after I got out of prison was a steep uphill climb. But once I was working with creatures who deal with hills for a living, I worked at it a little harder. I tried to sensitize myself to hear the things she wasn't outright saying but was signaling to me. And I learned how to bridge our present-day differences by connecting more deeply to our shared memories.

Likewise, with her new man, Paxton, I had to invent a whole new way of connecting if I was ever going to be part of Cassie's life. Here, too, I worked harder to attune myself to the frequencies he vibed at. Long story short, there's a reason that P and I have our best "conversations" when shooting down video-game zombies together (sorry, Hope!). And obviously, we didn't have memories together, but once I made an effort to sniff out the Scott Lang he was used to thinking about (in a nutshell, *a criminal*), I could consciously become the opposite of that.

As for Cassie, I've worked at both my sensitivity to her vibrations and drawn on our past together, and I can confidently report that . . . I still need help! Hank, if you're reading this, can you get to work on a Young Adult Communication Device?

Finally, what I dig so much about ants is their strength. Now this is the fun fact people usually get to first with ants. Depending on who you ask, ants can lift anywhere from fifty to five thousand times their body weight.

And yes, the Ant-Man suit replicates some of that, at both ends of the scale. Which is absolutely indispensable for battle and breaking into things. I'm still impressed at how Hank found a way for someone to be ant-sized but retain the proportional strength to punch like a human. Likewise, when I'm big, the suit gives me disproportionately greater strength than a guy that size. I've still got the outstanding airport repair bills to prove it.

However, even these totally badass mecha add-ons can

take a very heavy toll on the suit-wearer's own personal reserve of strength. When I enter giant mode, I'm the opposite of Captain America: I can do that for, well, not all day.

Which is why, ultimately, while the amplified force I can wield when Antified comes from the suit, it's not what keeps me going. Instead, I get the strength to keep fighting by drawing on the more important ant-qualities I've been talking about. The feelings of being part of a team and knowing others are depending on me give me a burst of purpose that powers me through. And along the same lines, those heightened senses of being more attuned to others, in all their complexity and dimensions, makes the battle more real for me. Because I know—and not only know, I feel and remember—who exactly it is I'm battling for.

So thanks, little guys, for looking out for this big one. We could all stand to learn a thing or three from how you work together and care for each other. And also, thanks for taking me in and letting a big clumsy primate crash the already very successful "ant party" you've got going on without us.

FAAMQ

Q: *What was the Quantum Realm like?*

A: Wow. Where do I begin? No, literally—it's pretty hard knowing where *anything* begins or ends there. Imagine a place of just "no rules." Up is down. Things just kinda "float" in the air. Shapes and colors you've never seen in nature commingle. Objects that seem alive are part of the landscape, while others that look like geological features move. I'm not a person who ingests substances, but it's enough to make you think you have.

But to be fair, I only spent what felt like five hours there, most of them focusing all my attention on trying to escape and screaming, "HOOOOPE!" If you want a more thorough answer, I'd ask Janet Van Dyne. But be warned: She sort of refuses to talk about it for some reason. Maybe because, after spending thirty years there, she's like, "Been there, done . . . whatever *that* was."

SUNDAY IN THE LAB WITH HANK

IF YOU'VE FOLLOWED MY story at all (and by the way, the beginning of this book would be a great place to start!) you'll know that most of my size-shifting adventures begin with a scientist named Hank Pym. He's a man whose mind is always seeking what's beyond the horizon. And I can't wait to see where it's likely to lead us next.

So I thought I'd have a little chat with Hank. Even though he's retired from his company, Hank Pym's mind cannot and will never retire. He stays out of Hope's way while she runs Pym Van Dyne Industries, but he's also set up his own private lab. And he still has *many* opinions about science, his discoveries, and the future.

Unfortunately (for me, not for the world), Hank is also just as much of a workaholic as ever. When I asked for fifteen minutes of his time, his first reply was, "That's fifteen minutes away from the lab."

Fortunately, I hashed out a compromise. Hank would let me (briefly) interview him while he was at work in the lab—as long as I didn't get too specific about what he's working on. That last part required some paperwork.

It's not usual practice to make the guy dating your daughter sign an NDA so big it looks like it's been enlarged with Pym Particles. But then again, by now, I'm pretty used to the unusual.

I started by asking Hank about something I'd wondered about recently after surviving a particularly nasty stomach bug.

Until now, Pym Particles have primarily been used to change the size of regular-sized things—me and you, a toy tank, an ant with dreams of being a rock drummer. But why not also use them to make *really* little things big? Things you can only see under a microscope: amoebas, germs, viruses . . . So we can see them much better and study them.

He reminded me that many germs and viruses are potentially lethal. No need, Hank! That stomach bug left me rattled enough to remember that. But he was making the point that making small dangerous things into bigger dangerous things can be . . . dangerous.

"Of course, a virus enlarged to the size of a grapefruit could be extremely valuable to virologists," Hank said. "But what if increasing its size also increases its ability to cause damage? What if it slips out of our control—and decides to attack us?"

Yikes. For someone who's gotten attacked by as many unexpected, dangerous things as the original Ant-Man Hank Pym has, that was no minor concern.

Here's a shot Hope took of Hank introducing me to the enlarging and shrinking discs he invented. It's all in the wrist.

"So what about tiny particles that aren't dangerous?" I tried. "The building-block stuff all life is made of: atoms, electrons, the quark's the limit!"

Possibly safer, Hank admitted. But he also pointed out something Janet Van Dyne (aka The Former Wasp, Hank's wife, and Hope's mom) and I have learned from tough personal experience: The Quantum Realm—where all those little building blocks live—can be wildly unpredictable. We'd barely gotten Janet out of there alive. We were not exactly prepared for an immediate return trip to that subatomic jungle!

In the meantime, all that tiny-thinking had brought me to nanotech. Obviously, Pym Van Dyne isn't the only lab experimenting with this groundbreaking, fascinating, and *really* hard-to-see new field. But I had a different notion of what PVD could accomplish than anyone else could.

"What do you think of nano *tools*?" I ventured. "Say you build a piece of equipment designed for a highly specific purpose at a normal scale—then reduce it to fit inside an artery, or a capillary, or even a cell."

Reader, I hope you're sitting down for what I'm about to relate next. . . .

Hank actually liked my idea.

Well, to be precise, he didn't hate it. His specific words were, "At least when we modify something that we ourselves built, we get to control the variables."

Trust me: For Hank Pym, that's practically gushing.

Emboldened by this opening, I decided to go straight for the most out-there idea I'd thought of.

"You know how a lot of people are working from home these days? What if we could use Pym Particles to better accommodate those workers by miniaturizing the whole office, or even the whole office building? You could have it travel around to key employees' homes, shrinking and expanding as needed. Imagine what kinds of startup businesses could get off the ground if they didn't have to invest in pricey, centrally located real estate."

Hank could have said a lot of things in response to that. Instead, as usual choosing as few words as he could to get me off his back and back to work, he opted for these:

"Remember what happened when I tried that with my lab?"

Indeed, I still had the asphalt burns from sprinting around San Francisco to remind me. Then Hank admitted it actually wasn't the worst idea he'd been pitched. It just wasn't an idea for . . . *now*.

That was actually the perfect segue to my next question, which I happen to think of as *extremely* "now," and I know this is one of Hope's priorities as the head of Pym Van Dyne Industries: the environment.

I asked Hank about the possibility of using Pym Particle technology to reduce the actual physical size of toxins in our air and water.

He replied, "Interesting." Again with the gushing, Hank!

Then he explained the complication. "In the real world, when you target something with a reducer, you have to shrink *the whole* something. So if you want to, say, reduce the pollution in a cubic meter of water, what you end up doing is *reducing that entire mass*. All the molecules, even the good ones, just get shrunk into a little ice cube."

But what about designing that reducer more precisely, to avoid the good molecules?

For Hank, this notion was on the table, but it took us back to the issue from earlier: the unpredictability of working in the subatomic space. In other words, this was the kind of thing Pym Van Dyne certainly wanted to crack, but we were still too much in "Unintended Consequences Land" to broach it yet.

Fair enough. I tried another tack, asking him about attacking an ecological problem that *does* have a consistent physical presence at human scale. For instance, we know as the planet gets hotter, our deserts are growing at an alarming pace. Could we use Pym Particles to shrink those deserts down?

Hank shot back, "Think about what you're doing when you apply reduction to a desert. You're not just shrinking down sand dunes. You're shrinking an entire rich and vibrant ecosystem. Do we really want to do that to a whole stratum of plants, animals, and insects?"

He had a point. And I'm pretty sure some of my ant pals aren't really eager to go any smaller.

But Hank wasn't done. "And even if, let's say, you could isolate a patch of desert where not too much flora and fauna would be affected. And you did make it smaller. According to some of our preliminary findings in terrestrial topology, that reduction might 'pull in' the land around it."

"Wow," I said, never even having considered this before. "Pretty sure our planet is not ready for 'global shrinking.'"

In the uncomfortable but all-too-familiar silence that followed my joke attempt, I thought of my final question.

"How does Pym Van Dyne Industries decide where to focus its resources? When you're choosing experiments, how do you separate what we humans actually *need* versus what we just *can do*?"

Here Hank did the unthinkable and actually stopped his work. Briefly. As with his technology, he wanted to make sure to get this right.

Finally, he spoke. And as before, he said something that seemed shocking but in fact made perfect sense:

Hank remarked that even though we could work on practically anything, ultimately, people might not really *want* many more options on resizing things. We humans tend to like our things predictable, familiar. And of course, we've spent tens of millions of years evolving to be best suited to this exact size and scale.

"Look, here's the bottom line," Hank concluded. "Before we blow things wide open and start planning what sizes everything in creation *could* be, maybe we need a better grasp on our own limitations as a species!"

Wow. Chills. That is *so* Hank Pym.

At this point, I really did want nothing more than to give the guy his work time back. Especially now that I'd just gained even more appreciation for his thoughtfulness. By way of wrapping up, I tried to express that. I praised Hank for recognizing how Pym Particles can be used for ill—even walking away from a lucrative career over it. And how that conscientiousness has always stuck with me, in all the situations he's put me into.

And then, only then, did Hank Pym drop his ultimate bombshell:

"Actually, son, seems like you've picked up on it pretty

well, too. Other than Janet or Hope, there's no one I trust more with my tech."

Then Hank gave his trademark nano-sized grin and gently pushed me outside the lab so he could close the door, as I stood there, still reeling from that, totally speechless.

In other words, once again Hank Pym had me exactly where he wanted me.

FAAMQ

Q: *Would you be willing to auction off a date with you for our charity?*

A: How flattering! I do like to help out whenever I can for a good cause. I'd love to!

However, just some fair warning: Beyond the fact that I'm still with Hope, I am *lousy* on a date! I've never been truly comfortable on a date with a woman, and it certainly didn't help to have all those years of enforced celibacy. (But enough about college!)

And beyond that, when you work in the hero trade, you become super-attuned to even the slightest hint of possible danger. Which could pretty much hijack any date. Let's say we're having a nice chat about our respective travails at work and what we're both binge-watching these days—and then someone in the vicinity starts trying some bad stuff. . . .

Goodbye, shared plate of cannoli, and hello, neighborhood trattoria getting turned into a smoke-filled battleground.

It's why I mostly get takeout.

A LETTER TO MY DAUGHTER

(THAT FOR SOME REASON *YOU PEOPLE* ARE ALSO READING)

MY DEAREST CASSIE (AKA "PEANUT"),

Hi! It's your dad.

Well, you know, your bio-dad. Not Paxton, who I have to admit is doing a hell of a job being there for you when I'm not around.

This is already getting awkward.

And maybe that's because we've been robbed of so much time together. So much time. Basically, half your life. Which makes me want to rush in and say all the things I couldn't say to you when I was in prison and

Cassie, I know you're going to hate that I put all these kid photos of you in my book—but I can't help but still think of you this way.

then trapped in the Quantum Realm all those years.

But instead, I'm going to try to just focus on the important stuff: some advice on how to make the most of your life.

I know, I know. Why should you—why should anyone—take life advice from a guy who's been arrested multiple times and spent three years in prison?

So right off the bat, that's my first piece of advice: Don't do that.

But also, say what you will about some of my . . . choices. You can't deny that I'm a person who's *lived*. So the least

I can do is turn all that unnecessary, crazy-making stuff I've gone through into something useful for you.

In my relatively short life, I've seen so much creation and destruction that, ironically, I've actually gotten a pretty good handle on the things that stick around long enough to matter.

So here's my take on what truly endures in this world and this life.

1. TIME MATTERS

I know what you're thinking: *"Oh look, here's my dad of all people telling me, 'You can't change a timeline!'"*

But look: Outside of the context of an epic adventure to save the universe, this is not really an option. And not only because the Pyms would be mad at either of us for using up any more of those particles. But also because as we Avengers learned, time heists can be *extremely* messy.

Which, in a strange way, actually kind of makes my point for me: *Don't mess around with time!*

We ordinary mortals are given a finite amount of it, and we can either waste it or maximize every second of it.

I say, "Maximize."

I know, this probably sounds cliché to you—or even worse, irrelevant. And I get it. You're young and you're feeling immortal. And, to use another cliché that everyone's undoubtedly throwing at you all the time, "You have your whole life ahead of you."

But that's the tricky part. Pretty soon, you're going to find out that you actually may not "have" all that life to yourself. Jobs will gobble up your precious time. People will need you. Circumstances will constrain you. Enemies—personal, institutional, biological—may arise out of nowhere to suck whatever time-dregs are left. I still can't believe which decade of life I'm already in.

So right now, while you still have some nominal say in where your life goes from here, fight for every scrap of it.

Also, to take on one more cliché (last one, I promise!), you know the one that goes "There's no time like the present"?

Lies.

Take it from someone who's literally experimented with timelines: There is no time *but* the present! Everything you want to do, everyone you want to be, and everyone you want to be with—chase all that down *today*!

Don't wait, because trust me, none of it will wait for you.

About now you might be thinking, "*But, Dad*, you *went away. And I did wait. And then, you came back. Twice!*"

Yes, of course that's true. But I also don't think I need to remind you of all the things you and I missed out on sharing during those times, which we definitely are not getting back:

- walking you to your first day of "big girl" school
- your "Unicorns vs. Dragons" fourth birthday party
- your debut on stage as "Tap-Dancing Tree #3"

If you think I would have been a blubbering mess at any of those moments (Spoiler Alert: I would have), just imagine how wrecked I was having to imagine them while sitting on a hard cot in my cold, lonely cell. I don't want to alarm you, but it was prison. My life *was* in danger. And yet, the only life I was thinking of during those moments was yours, going on without me in it.

And you must remember those nights when I'd just gotten back from the Quantum Realm. Looking through the photo album together, poring over the endless, smiling faces of people who suddenly got yanked out of our lives. And, in the worst possible reversal of how things are supposed to go between parents and kids, you were the one wiping my tears and telling me, "It's okay, it's okay."

Now that I look back on such moments, I wasn't just in mourning for people we'd lost. I was also mourning all the time you and I had lost.

No amount of Pym Particles or Infinity Stones could turn those lost memories (for me) into shared memories (for us). What I do know is that there will be more memories that you will make to share with others—but only if you take action today and make them happen.

So, bottom line: Seize the tap-dancing battle-unicorn, Cassie!

2. SIZE MATTERS

I know: *"Easy for you to say, Mr. I-Can-Literally-Change-My-Size-At-Will."* But again, I want to turn my weird life journey into your advantage.

First, being big gives a person a whole different perspective on life. They start to see all those massive streets, buildings, and cities that we humans create and get so intimidated by as nothing but toy structures, temporary obstacles on their ultimate path.

And also, from that perspective, people start to look like, well, ants. Which can be a remarkably liberating feeling. We spend so much of our time operating in fear of other people—of their judgments, their regard, their powerful emotions. But at the end of the day, they really don't have the power to make or break us—no matter how they may act when we're all the same size.

What I learned from being Giant Dad is that the only people who should be huge in your life are those whom you choose to have in your life. I know you felt how big the gap was when your friends and loved ones got blipped away for five years. So now that they're back, make sure they know now how much they fill those gaps in for you—like, every day.

Meanwhile, from the other side of the scale, I can also tell you what being small has taught me.

And it's basically that, in a nutshell, the little things really add up. In Ant World, a crumb of focaccia could be the key to a week's survival. Likewise, in Human World, a kind word or a cruel one can transform someone's entire day.

Seeing the world at tiny scale makes a person truly appreciate all the tiny things—the things we too often overlook. It makes me mindful of the infinitude of miracles holding everything we care about together. It's enough to make me truly grateful.

And trust me: Gratitude can give you more strength and energy than any power source in the galaxy.

So don't lose sight of the small stuff, because that's the true reality of the world.

But also . . . contradiction alert . . .

3. SIZE *DOESN'T* MATTER

What do I mean by this? What I mean is: Never let yourself get defined by anyone else's notions of how "big" or "small" you are in their eyes. You alone decide your size, with or without a fancy red size-changing button.

And that also means you—and nobody else—are in charge of deciding when to make yourself "big" or "small" in any given situation. Be big when speaking up against an unfair boss, a disrespectful partner, and an unjust government or corporation. I've already seen you doing some of this, and I couldn't be prouder. But be careful—the last thing we need is two Langs spending time behind bars!

And also: Be small enough to admit fault, as well as what you don't know and need to learn.

From what I've seen of the young woman you're becoming, I know I don't need to drill you in martial arts like Hope's dad did for her. You already know how to fight. You've been doing it your whole life.

But if nothing else I've put down here has made it through, I just want to convey one idea to you: *You already have the power to become the size you want.*

And that's what, my darling Peanut—of whatever size you want to be—I want most in this world to leave to you.

BIG (and also small) love,

Dad

SIZING IT ALL UP

I'VE HAD A WEIRD life. And I wouldn't trade away a second of it.

Well, okay, maybe the three years of it when I was in prison. But then I wouldn't have met Luis. Or come to Hank Pym's attention. And Hope's . . .

Okay, then maybe those five years of the world I missed when I was spending what seemed like five hours in the Quantum Realm. But then again, without those five year-hours, I wouldn't have come up with the idea that got everyone back from the Blip and helped beat Thanos.

So, in my usual Scott Lang roundabout way, this is kind of my point:

You never really know which moments of your life will turn out to be the ones that mean the most. So you might as well embrace all of them!

Because, if you think about it, we all experience the passage of time in our own lives. Or at least we feel like we do. How it seems to rush by too fast when we're having fun or watching our kids grow; or drag on too slowly when we're getting our teeth cleaned or hearing our officemate tell us about his crazy dream last night.

What I mean is, we're all capable of traveling across the vast range of time in our lives, using only our minds. As far as I know, we're the only species that can do this in a sustained and meaningful way. Even my awesome ant-buddies are really only capable of present-tense-oriented thinking, which makes sense, considering their collective mentality.

But the point is, we humans—all humans—have been given this very unique power to mentally liberate ourselves from our present moment. So what do we *do* with that? That's the cool part. We're all ultimately the authors of our own story. Of course I don't mean we get to determine our own outcome. But we do get to decide something ultimately even more precious:

What every beat of our story *means*.

Ultimately, that was my purpose in writing this book. I mean, besides my buddies asking me to. As I've dug back into all the things that have happened to me, I've come to believe that every moment of it has been for a reason. How can I be so sure? Because I have it within me—just as you do—to *give* it a reason. By using it to inform the many moments to come. You might say we all have an origin story, and that story is always still being told.

In these pages, I've tried to tell my story, but not just the marquee bits that'll end up in my obit when I head for that Big Anthill in the Sky. I've attempted to figure out how not just those moments, but also—especially!—the "ordinary" moments surrounding them shaped who I am today.

And you can do the same.

Now just to be clear, having our lives mean something isn't the same as having it all make sense.

Because if I think about it, my life doesn't really make sense. I used to ask myself a lot of questions about that. "Scott, you're a divorced ex-con, how are you an Avenger? Why are you time traveling with Captain America? That doesn't make sense."

Well, they're right. It doesn't make sense. Because

what I've learned is, it's not up to other people or forces to "make sense" for us. We have to make it ourselves.

A lot has changed about my life. But everywhere I go, people ask me the same thing: "Scott, what about now? What's next? Where does the ride take you?"

Hank took this photo as a record of my early training. He thankfully did not feel the need to document all the times my training involved me throwing up.

Who knows? If I knew that . . . it wouldn't be a ride. But the one thing I do know is, wherever the ride takes you, you will not be riding alone.

It's been a crazy few years. For everyone. So let's make time for the stuff that really matters. Like friends—friends you didn't even know you had. Remember the people who got you here; you couldn't have done it without them.

Trust me on this: No one you've ever crossed paths with is too "little" to be worth a moment of your time and, in some cases, appreciation. I should know. I'm just a guy who got fired from Baskin-Robbins.

But thanks to someone else, nowadays I'm also something besides that.

I'm a little guy who was taken notice of. Even if it was just to use my criminal skills. Hank's recognition of what even I, an ex-con divorcé absentee-dad failed ice-cream scooper, was still capable of contributing to the world has made all the difference. As has the woman he happens to be the father of.

What can I say? Sometimes you just get lucky. I'm lucky I met Hope Van Dyne. I think you know who she is by now. She's taken back her dad's company. Now she's using the Pym Particle for global change. A lot of people say they want to save the world. But Hope—she saves it every day. Reforestation. Affordable housing. Food production. She's not wasting a second.

I still can't believe it; none of this should have happened. But it did.

One thing I admire most about Hope and her work is how she's not sitting back, wondering how bad things could have gone differently. She's taking charge and making change. Hope is racing ahead to fix future things now. She's moved on in a way that I'm still struggling to do.

And don't get me wrong: It's not that I'm trapped in negativity. Sure, our planet will continue to face threats and problems. But on the whole, it's a pretty good world. I'm glad we saved it.

So that brings me to . . . now. As in, "What do I with it?" Great question. I'll let you know as soon as I know the answer.

Do I miss the action? Sometimes. Will I be there when the Avengers need me? Absolutely. I'd never turn my back on them. But right now, the only job I want is being a dad.

Which brings me to the person this book is really aimed at. Or at least the person whom I just wanted to say something to:

I love you, Cassie. Thank you for being my hero.

And I'm sorry I missed some birthdays.

And for the rest of you kids out there, a word of advice: Look out for the little guy. Make mistakes. Take chances. Because if there's one thing life's taught me, there's always . . . room to grow.

ACKNOWLEDGMENTS

If you read the whole book that came before these acknowledgments, you probably know the first people I want to thank: Cassie, Hope, Hank, Janet, Luis, Maggie, and Paxton. You're the best reasons I've ever had to come back from the Quantum Realm. Also, I'm going to go ahead and thank the Avengers (you know who you are) for saving the world, and for asking me to write this book (not necessarily in that order).

There are also some people you didn't read about in this book, but who were Very Important in helping a certain guy who never ever thought he'd write a book to somehow actually write a book. First and most important is Rob Kutner, who was with me every step of the way as my writing coach, cheerleader, late-night texter, transcriber, and even occasional crying partner. (We must never, ever discuss with anyone else the secret confessions we shared with each other that night, Rob. Remember, my ant minions are always watching you.) This book would literally not have been written without Rob.

There were a bunch of key people on the Avengers side of things who made sure I didn't spell Thanos with two *n*'s (I only ever heard it spoken aloud!) and also got all my other facts right. (If I didn't, that is definitely on me, not them.) They are: Kristy Amornkul, Natalie Artin, Andrew Baron-Vartian, Sara Truly Beers, Stephen Broussard, Capri Ciulla, Adam Davis, Andrea Lans, Sven Larsen, Kelly Li, Molly Jones, Rachel Paige, Julio Palacol, Ron Richards, Jacqueline Ryan-Rudolph, Sarah Singer, Jenny Moussa Spring, and Matt Wilkie. I've learned that behind every super-team, there is another just as super super-team.

At my publisher, Hyperion Avenue, a group of super-powered wordsmiths, designers, copy editors, proofreaders, and bookmakers gathered all these letters and lines and dots together and got 'em printed on bound-together sheets of paper, and also let the world know about it. I'm looking at you, Tonya Agurto, Danna Bremer, Catalina Castro, Guy Cunningham, Monique Diman-Riley, Lisa M. Geller, Daneen Goodwin, Kurt Hartman, Soyoung Kim, Amy King, Vicki Korlishin, Kaitie Leary, Anthony J. Lee, Jennifer Levesque, Sara Liebling, John Morgan, Scott Piehl, Carol Roeder, Alexandra Serrano, Fanny Sheffield, Michael Siglain, Stephanie Sumulong, Gegham Vardanyan, Lynn Waggoner, Beth Wasko, and Tyneka A. Woods. And I'm sure there are many others I'm forgetting or who were better than the people listed here at avoiding having to deal directly with me.

Finally, I want to acknowledge you, the person who read this book, or at least these acknowledgments, or at least this sentence. I still can't believe all these amazing things happened to me, and my goal in writing this book (with a lot of help from Rob) was to give you a sense of what it would feel like if they'd happened to you, and what you'd learn from them. I never thought I'd get a chance to communicate with another person that way, and I'm only able to because you picked up a book with me on the cover and decided to give it a read. So thank you, little guy. I'm looking out for you.

MARVEL STUDIOS' ANT-MAN, *CAPTAIN AMERICA: CIVIL WAR, ANT-MAN AND THE WASP,* AND *AVENGERS: ENDGAME* ARE AVAILABLE NOW IN DIGITAL AND PHYSICAL FORMATS WHEREVER MOVIES ARE SOLD, AND ARE ALSO STREAMING ON DISNEY+.